THE CAMPFIRE GIRLS
OF ROSELAWN

The
CAMPFIRE GIRLS
of Roselawn

OR

A STRANGE MESSAGE
FROM THE AIR

• •
•

By Margaret Penrose

WILDSIDE PRESS

CONTENTS

CONTENTS

They Hear a Voice

THE CAMPFIRE GIRLS OF ROSELAWN

CHAPTER I

THEY HEAR A VOICE

"OH, it's wonderful, Amy! Just wonderful!"

The blonde girl in the porch swing looked up with shining eyes and flushed face from her magazine to look at the dark girl who swung composedly in a rocking chair, her nimble fingers busy with the knitting of a shoulder scarf. The dark girl bobbed her head in agreement.

"So's the Sphinx, but it's awfully out of date, Jess."

Jessie Norwood looked offended. "Did I ever bring to your attention, Miss Drew——"

"Why don't you say 'drew' to my attention?" murmured the other girl.

"Because I perfectly loathe puns," declared Jessie, with energy.

"Good! Miss Seymour's favorite pupil. Go on about the wonder beast, Jess."

"It is no beast, I'd have you understand. And it is right up to date—the very newest thing."

"My dear Jessie," urged her chum, gayly, "you have tickled my curiosity until it positively wriggles! What is the wonder?"

"Radio!"

"Oh! Wireless?"

"Wireless telephone. Everybody is having one."

"Grandma used to prescribe sulphur and molasses for that."

"Do be sensible for once, Amy Drew. You and Darry——"

"That reminds me. Darry knows all about it."

"About what?"

"The radio telephone business. You know he was eighteen months on a destroyer in the war, even if he was only a kid. You know," and Amy giggled, "he says that if women's ages are always elastic, it was no crime for him to stretch his age when he enlisted. Anyhow, he knows all about the 'listening boxes' down in the hold. And that is all this radio is."

"Oh, but Amy!" cried Jessie, with a toss of her blond head, "that is old stuff. The radio of to-day is very different—much improved. Anybody can have a receiving set and hear the most wonderful things out of the air. It has been brought to every home."

" 'Have you a little radio in your home?' "
chuckled Amy, her fingers still flying.

"Dear me, Amy, you are so difficult," sighed
her chum.

"Not at all, not at all," replied the other girl.
"You can understand me, just as e-e-easy! But
you know, Jess, I have to act as a brake for your
exuberance."

"Don't care," declared Jessie. "I'm going to
have one."

"If cook isn't looking, bring one for me, too,"
suggested the irrepressible joker.

"I mean to have a radio set," repeated Jessie
quite seriously. "It says in this magazine article
that one can erect the aerials and all, oneself. And
place the instrument. I am going to do it."

"Sure you can," declared Amy, with confidence.
"If you said you could rebuild the Alps—and improve on them—I'd root for you, honey."

"I don't want any of your joking," declared
Jessie, with emphasis. "I am in earnest."

"So am I. About the Alps. Aunt Susan, who
went over this year, says the traveling there is
just as rough as it was before the war. She
doesn't see that the war did any good. If I were
you, Jess, and thought of making over the
Alps——"

"Now, Amy Drew! Who said anything about
the Alps?"

"I did," confessed her chum. "And I was about to suggest that, if you tackle the job of rebuilding them, you flatten 'em out a good bit so Aunt Susan can get across them easier."

"Amy Drew! Will you ever have sense?"

"What is it, a conundrum? Something about 'Take care of the dollars and the cents will take care of themselves?'"

"I am talking about installing a radio set in our house. And if you don't stop funning and help me do it, I won't let you listen in, so there!"

"I'll be good," proclaimed Amy at once. "I enjoy gossip just as much as the next one. And if you can get it out of the air——"

"It has to be sent from a broadcasting station," announced Jessie.

"There's one right in this town," declared Amy, with vigor.

"No!"

"Yes, I tell you. She lives in the second house from the corner of Breen Street, the yellow house with green blinds——"

"Now, Amy! Listen here! Never mind local gossips. They only broadcast neighborhood news. But we can get concerts and weather reports and lectures——"

Amy painfully writhed in her chair at this point. "Say not so, Jess!" she begged. "Get lectures enough at school—and from dad, once in a while, when the dear thinks I go too far."

"I think you go too far most of the time," declared her chum primly. "Nobody else would have the patience with you that I have."

"Except Burd Alling," announced Amy composedly. "He thinks I am all right."

"Pooh! Whoever said Burd Alling had good sense?" demanded Jessie. "Now listen!" She read a long paragraph from the magazine article. "You see, it is the very latest thing to do. Everybody is doing it. And it is the most wonderful thing!"

Amy had listened with more seriousness. She could be attentive and appreciative if she wished. The paragraph her chum read was interesting.

"Go ahead. Read some more," she said. "Is that all sure enough so, Jess?"

"Of course it is so. Don't you see it is printed here?"

"You mustn't believe everything you see in print, Jess. My grandfather was reported killed in the Civil War, and he came home and pointed out several things they had got wrong in the newspaper obituary—especially the date of his demise. Now this——"

"I am going to get a book about it, and that will tell us just what to do in getting a radio set established."

"I'll tell you the first thing to do," scoffed Amy. "Dig down into your pocketbook."

"It won't cost much. But I mean to have a good one."

"All right, dear. I am with you. Never let it be said I deserted Poll. What is the first move?"

"Now, let me see," murmured Jessie, staring off across the sunflecked lawn.

The Norwood estate was a grand place. The house, with its surrounding porches, stood in Rose-lawn upon a knoll with several acres of sloping sod surrounding it and a lovely little lake at the side. There was a long rose garden on either side of the house, and groups of summer roses in front. Roses, roses, roses, everywhere about the place! The Norwoods all loved them.

But there were more roses in this section of the pretty town of New Melford, and on that account many inhabitants of the place had gotten into the habit of calling the estates bordering the boule-vard by the name of Roselawn. It was the Rose-lawn district, for every lawn was dotted with roses, red, pink, white, and yellow.

The Norwoods were three. Jessie, we put first because to us she is of the most importance, and her father and mother would agree. Being the only child, it is true they made much of her. But Jessie Norwood was too sweet to be easily spoiled.

Her father was a lawyer in New York, which

was twenty miles from New Melford. The Norwoods had some wealth, which was good. They
had culture, which was better. And they were a
very loving and companionable trio, which was
best.

Across the broad, shaded boulevard was a
great, rambling, old house, with several broad
chimneys. It had once been a better class farm-
stead. Mr. Wilbur Drew, who was likewise a
lawyer, had rebuilt and added to and improved
and otherwise transformed the farmhouse until
it was an attractive and important-looking
dwelling.

In it lived the lawyer and his wife, his daughter,
Amy, and Darrington Drew, when he was home
from college. This was another happy family—
in a way. Yet they were just a little different
from the Norwoods. But truly "nice people."

When Amy Drew once gave her mind to a
thing she could be earnest enough. The little her
chum had read her from the magazine article
began to interest her. Besides, whatever Jessie
was engaged in must of necessity hold the attention of Amy.

She laid aside the knitting and went to sit
beside Jessie in the swing. They turned back to
the beginning of the article and read it through
together, their arms wound about each other in
immemorial schoolgirl fashion.

Of course, as Amy pointed out, they were not exactly schoolgirls now. They were out of school —since two days before. The long summer vacation was ahead of them. Time might hang idly on their hands. So it behooved them to find something absorbing to keep their attention keyed up to the proper pitch.

"Tell you what," Amy suggested. "Let's go down town to the bookstore and see if they have laid in a stock of this radio stuff. We want one or two of the books mentioned here, Jess. We are two awfully smart girls, I know; we will both admit it. But some things we have positively got to learn."

"Silly," crooned Jessie, patting her chum on the cheek. "Let's go. We'll walk. Wait till I run and see if Momsy doesn't want something from down town."

"We won't ask Mrs. Drew that question, for she will be pretty sure to want a dozen things, and I refuse—positively—to be a dray horse. I 'have drew' more than my share from the stores already. Cyprian in the car can run the dear, forgetful lady's errands."

Jessie scarcely listened to this. She ran in and ran out again. She was smiling.

"Momsy says all she wants is two George Washington sundaes, to be brought home in two separate parcels, one blonde and one brunette," and she held up half a dollar before Amy's eyes.

"Your mother, as I have always said, Jess, is of the salt of the earth. And she is well sugared, too. Let me carry the half dollar, honey. You'll swallow it, or lose it, or something. Aren't to be trusted yet with money," and Amy marched down the steps in the lead.

She always took the lead, and usually acted as though she were the moving spirit of the pair. But, really, Jessie Norwood was the more practical, and it was usually her initiative that started the chums on a new thing and always her "stick-toitiveness" that carried them through to the end.

Bonwit Boulevard, beautifully laid out, shaded with elms, with a grass path in the middle, two oiled drives, and with a bridle path on one side, was one of the finest highways in the state. At this hour of the afternoon, before the return rush of the auto-commuters from the city, the road was almost empty.

The chums chatted of many things as they went along. But Jessie came back each time to radio. She had been very much interested in the wonder of it and in the possibility of rigging the necessary aerials and setting up a receiving set at her own house.

"We can get the books to tell us how to do it, and we can buy the wire for the antenna to-day," she said.

" 'Antenna'! Is it an insect?" demanded Amy. "Sounds crawly."

"Those are the aerials——"

"Listen!" interrupted Amy Drew.

A sound—a shrill and compelling voice—reached their ears. Amy's hand clutched at Jessie's arm and held her back. There was nobody in sight, and the nearest house was some way back from the road.

"What is it?" murmured Jessie.

"Help! He-e-elp!" repeated the voice, shrilly.

"Radio!" muttered Amy, sepulchrally. "It is a voice out of the air."

There positively was nobody in sight. But Jessie Norwood was practical. She knew there was a street branching off the boulevard just a little way ahead. Besides, she heard the throbbing of an automobile engine.

"Help!" shrieked the unknown once more.

"It is a girl," declared Jessie, beginning to run and half dragging Amy Drew with her. "She is in trouble! We must help her!"

A Road Mystery

CHAPTER II

L IKE a great many other beautiful streets, there was a poverty-stricken section, if sparsely inhabited, just behind Bonwit Boulevard. A group of shacks and squatters' huts down in a grassy hollow, with a little brook flowing through it to the lake, and woods beyond. It would not have been an unsightly spot if the marks of the habitation of poor and careless folk had been wiped away.

But at the moment Jessie Norwood and her chum, Amy Drew, darted around from the broad boulevard into the narrow lane that led down to this poor hamlet, neither of the girls remembered "Dogtown," as the group of huts was locally called. The real estate men who exploited Rose-lawn and Bonwit Boulevard as the most aristocratic suburban section of New Melford, never spoke of Dogtown.

"What do you suppose is the matter, Jess?" panted Amy.

"It's a girl in trouble! Look at that!"

The chums did not have to go even as far as the brow of the hill overlooking the group of houses before mentioned. The scene of the action of this drama was not a hundred yards off the boulevard.

A big touring car stood in the narrow lane, headed toward the broad highway from which Jessie and Amy had come. It was a fine car, and the engine was running. A very unpleasant look-ing, narrow-shouldered woman sat behind the steering wheel, but was twisted around in her seat so that she could look behind her.

In the lane was another woman. Both were expensively dressed, though not tastefully; and this second woman was as billowy and as gen-erously proportioned as the one behind the wheel was lean. She was red-faced, too, and panted from her exertions.

Those exertions, it was evident at once to Jessie and Amy, were connected with the captur-ing and the subsequent restraining of a very active and athletic girl of about the age of the chums. She was quite as red-faced as the fleshy woman, and she was struggling with all her might to get away, while now and then she emitted a shout for help that would have brought a crowd in almost no time in any place more closely built up.

"Oh! What is the matter?" repeated Amy.

"Bring her along, Martha!" exclaimed the woman already in the motor-car. "Here come a couple of rubber-necks."

This expression, to Jessie's mind, marked the

driver of the automobile for exactly what she was. Nor did the face of the fat woman impress the girl as being any more refined.

As for the girl struggling with the second woman—the one called "Martha"—she was not very well dressed. But she looked neat and clean, and she certainly was determined not to enter the automobile if she could help it. Jessie doubted, although she had at first thought it possible, if either of these women were related to the girl they seemed so determined to capture.

"What are they—road pirates? Kidnapers?" demanded Amy. "What?"

The two chums stopped by the machine. They really did not know what to do. Should they help the screaming girl? Or should they aid the fleshy woman? It might be that the girl had run away from perfectly good guardians. Only, to Jessie's mind, there was something of the refinement that pertained to the girl lacking in the appearance of these two women. She was not favorably impressed by them.

"What is the matter with the girl?" she asked the woman in the car.

Although she said it politely, the woman flashed her a scowling glance and said:

"Mind your own business!"

"My!" gasped Amy at this, her eyes opening very wide.

Jessie was not at all reassured. She turned to the fleshy woman, and repeated her question:

"What is the matter with the girl?"

"She's crazy, that's what she is!" cried the woman. "She doesn't know what is good for her."

"I'll learn her!" rasped out the driver of the car.

"Don't!" shouted the girl. "Don't let them take me back there——"

Just then the fleshy woman got behind her. She clutched the girl's shoulders and drove her harshly toward the car with her whole weight behind the writhing girl. The other woman jumped out of the car, seized the girl by one arm, and together the women fairly threw their captive into the tonneau of the car, where she fell on her hands and knees.

"There, spiteful!" gasped the lean woman. "I'll show you!"

She hopped back behind the steering wheel. The fleshy woman climbed into the tonneau and held the still shrieking girl. The car started with a dash, the door of the tonneau flapping.

"Oh! This isn't right!" gasped Jessie.

"They are running away with her, Jess," murmured Amy. "Isn't it exciting?"

"It's mean!" declared her chum with conviction. "How dare they?"

"Why, to look at her, I think that skinny woman would dare anything," remarked Amy. "And—haven't—you seen her before?"

"Never! She doesn't live around here. And that car is strange."

The car had turned into the boulevard and headed out of town. When the girls walked back to the broad highway it was out of sight. It was being driven with small regard for the speed laws.

"I guess you are right," reflected Amy. "I never saw that car before. It is a French car. But the woman's face——"

"There was enough of that to remember," declared Jessie, quite spitefully.

"I didn't mean the fat woman's face," giggled Amy. "I mean that the other woman looked familiar. Maybe I have seen her picture somewhere."

"If my face was like hers I'd never have it photographed," snapped Jessie.

"How vinegarish," said Amy. "Well, it was funny."

"You do find humor in the strangest things," returned her chum. "I guess that poor girl didn't think it was funny."

"Of course, they had some right to her," Amy declared.

"How do you know they did? They did not

act so," returned the more thoughtful Jessie. "If they had really the right to make the poor girl go with them, they would not have acted in such haste nor answered me the way they did."

"Well, of course, it wasn't any of our business either to ask questions or to interfere," Amy declared.

"I don't know about that, Amy," rejoined her chum. "I wish your brother had been here, or somebody."

"Darry!" scoffed Amy.

"Or maybe Burd Alling," and Jessie's eyes twinkled.

"Well," considered Amy demurely, "I suppose the boys might have known better what to do." .

"Oh," said Jessie, promptly, "I knew what to do, all right; only I couldn't do it."

"What is that?"

"Stopped the women and made them explain before we allowed them to take the girl away. And I wonder where she was going. When and where did she run away from the women? Did you hear her beg us not to let them take her back—back——"

"Back where?"

"That is it, exactly," sighed Jessie, as the two walked on toward town. "She did not tell us where."

"Some institution, maybe. An orphan asylum," suggested Amy.

"Did you think she looked like an orphan?"

"How does an orphan look?" giggled Amy. "I don't know any except the *Molly Mickford* kind in the movies, and they are always too appealing for words!"

"Somehow, she didn't look like that," admitted Jessie.

"She fought hard. I believe I would have scratched that fat woman's face myself, if I'd been her. Anyway, she wasn't in any uniform. Don't they always put orphans in blue denim?"

"Not always. And that girl would have looked awful in blue. She was too dark. She wasn't very well dressed, but her clothes and their colors were tasteful."

"Aren't you the observing thing," agreed Amy. "She was dressed nicely. And those women were never guards from an institution."

"Oh, no!"

"It was a private kidnaping party, I guess," said Amy.

"And we let it go on right under our noses and did not stop it," sighed Jessie Norwood. "I'm going to tell my father about it."

Amy grinned elfishly. "He will tell you that you had a right, under the law, to stop those women and make them explain."

"Ye-es. I suppose so. But a right to do a thing and the ability to do it, he will likewise tell me, are two very different things."

"Wisdom from the young owl!" laughed Amy. "Well, I don't suppose, after all, it is any of our business, or ever will be. The poor thing is now a captive and being borne away to the dungeon-keep. Whatever that is," she added, shrugging her shoulders.

Interest in Radio Spreads

CHAPTER III

INTEREST IN RADIO SPREADS

OVER the George Washington sundaes at the New Melford Dainties Shop the girls discussed the mysterious happening on Dogtown Lane until it was, as Amy said, positively frayed.

"We do not know what it was all about, my dear, so why worry our minds? We shall probably never see that girl again, or those two women. Only, that lean one—well! I know I have seen her somewhere, or somebody who looks like her."

"I don't see but you are just as bad as I am," Jessie Norwood said. "But we did not come to town because of that puzzling thing."

"No-o. We came to get these perfectly gorgeous sundaes," declared Amy Drew. "Your mother, Jess, is almost as nice as you are."

"We came in to get radio books and buy wire and stops and all that for the aerials, anyway. Of course, I shall have to send for most of the parts of the house set. There is no regular radio equipment dealer in New Melford."

"Oh, yes! Wireless!" murmured Amy. "I had almost forgotten that."

They trotted across the street to the bookstore. Motors were coming up from the station now, and from New York. They waved their hands to several motoring acquaintances, and just out-side Ye Craftsman's Bookshop they ran into Nell Stanley, who they knew had no business at all there on Main Street at this hour of the after-noon. Nell was the minister's daughter, and there were a number of little motherless Stanleys at the parsonage (Amy said "a whole raft of them") who usually needed the older sister's attention, approaching supper time.

"Oh, I've a holiday," laughed Nell, who was big and strong and really handsome, Jessie thought, her coloring was so fresh, her chestnut hair so abundant, her gray eyes so brilliantly in-telligent, and her teeth so dazzling. "Aunt Freda is at the house and she and the Reverend told me to go out and not to show myself back home for *hours.*"

"Bully-good!" declared Amy. "You'll come home to dinner with me, and we will spend the evening with Jess helping her build a radio thing so we can do without buying the New Melford *Tribune* to get the local news."

"Oh, Jess, dear, *are* you going to have a radio?" cried Nell. "It's just wonderful. Reverend says he may have to broadcast his sermons pretty soon or else be without an audience."

The pet name by which she usually spoke of her father, the Reverend Doctor Stanley, sounded all right when Nell said it. Nobody else ever called the good clergyman by it. But Nell was something between a daughter and a wife to the hard working Doctor Stanley. And she certainly was a thoughtful and "mothering" sister to the little ones.

"But," Nell added, "you are too late inviting me to the eats, Amy, honey. It can't be done. I'm promised. Mr. Brandon and his wife saw me first, and I am to dine with them. Then they are going to take me in their car out to the Parkville home of their daughter—Oh, say! If your radio isn't finished, Jess, why can't you and Amy come with us? The Brandon car is big enough. And they tell me Mrs. Brandon's daughter has got a perfectly wonderful set at her home. They have an amplifier, and you don't have to use phones at all. Has your radio set got an amplifier, Jess?"

"But I haven't got it yet," cried Jess. "I only hope to have it."

"Then you and Amy come and hear a real one," said Nell.

"If the Brandons won't mind. Will they?"

"You know they are the loveliest people," said

Nell briskly. "Mrs. Brandon told me to invite some young friends. But I hadn't thought of doing so. But I must have you and Amy. We'll be along for you girls at about seven-forty-five, new time."

"Then we must hurry," declared Jess, as the minister's daughter ran away.

"I'm getting interested," announced Amy. "Is this radio business like a talking machine?"

"Only better," said her chum. "Come on. I know several of the little books I want to get. I wrote down the names."

They dived down the four steps into the basement bookshop. It was a fine place to browse, when one had an hour to spare. But the chums from Roselawn were not in browsing mood on this occasion.

They knew exactly what they wanted—at least, Jessie Norwood did—and somewhat to their surprise right near the front door of the shop was a "radio table."

"Oh, yes, young ladies," said the clerk who came to wait upon them only when he saw that they had made their selections, "we have quite a call for books on that topic. It is becoming a fad, and quite wonderful, too. I have thought some of buying a radio set myself."

"We're going to build one," declared Amy with her usual prompt assurance.

"Are you? You two girls? Well, I don't
know why you shouldn't. Lots of boys are doing
so."

"And anything a boy can do a girl ought to do
a little better," Amy added.

The clerk laughed as he wrapped up the several books Jessie had charged to her father's account. "You let me know how you get on building
it, will you?" he said. "Maybe I can get some
ideas from your experience."

"We'll show 'em!" declared Amy, all in a glow
of excitement. "And why do you suppose, Jess,
folks always have to suggest that girls can't do
what boys can? Isn't it ridiculous!"

"Very," agreed Jessie. "Although, just as I
pointed out a while ago, it would have been handy
if Darry or Burd had been with us when we saw
that poor girl kidnaped."

"Of course! But, then, those boys are college
men." She giggled. "And I wager Burd is a
sea-sick college man just now."

"Oh! Have they gone out in the *Marigold?*"
cried Jessie.

"They left New Haven the minute they could
get away and joined the yacht at Groton, over
across from New London, where it has been tied
up all winter. Father insisted that Darry
shouldn't touch the yacht, when Uncle Will died
and left it to him last fall, until the college year

was ended. We got a marconigram last night that they had passed Block Island going out. And *now*—well, Burd never was at sea before, you know," and Amy laughed again.

"It has been rather windy. I suppose it must be rough out in the ocean. Oh, Amy!" Jess suddenly exclaimed, "if I get my radio rigged why can't we communicate with the *Marigold* when it is at sea?"

"I don't know just why you can't. But I guess the wireless rigging on the yacht isn't like this radio thing you are going to set up. They use some sort of telegraph alphabet."

"I know," declared Jessie with conviction. "I'll tell Darry to put in a regular sending set— like the one I hope to have, if father will let me. And we can have our two sets tuned so that we can hear each other speak."

"My goodness! You don't mean it is as easy as all that?" cried Amy.

"Didn't you read that magazine article?" demanded her chum. "And didn't the man say that, pretty soon, we could carry receiving and sending sets in our pockets—maybe—and stop right on the street and send or receive any news we wanted to?"

"No, I sha'n't," declared Amy. "Pockets spoil the set of even a sports skirt. Where you going now?"

"In here. Mr. Brill sells electrical supplies as
well as hardware. Oh! Amy Drew! There is a
radio set in his window! I declare, New Melford
is advancing in strides!"

"Sure! In seven league boots," murmured
Amy, following her friend into the store.

Jessie had noted down the things she thought
it would be safe to order before speaking to her
father about the radio matter. Mrs. Norwood
had cheerfully given her consent. Amy had once
said that if Jessie went to her mother and asked if
she could have a pet plesiosaurus, Mrs. Norwood
would say:

"Of course, you may, dear. But don't bring it
into the house when its feet are wet."

For the antenna and lead-in and ground wires,
Jessie purchased three hundred feet of copper
wire, number fourteen. The lightning switch Mr.
Brill had among his electric fixtures—merely a
porcelain base, thirty ampere, single pole double
throw battery switch. She also obtained the
necessary porcelain insulators and tubes.

She knew there would be plenty of rope in the
Norwood barn or the garage for their need in
erecting the aerials. But she bought a small
pulley as well as the ground connections which
Mr. Brill had in stock. He was anxious to sell
her a complete set like that he was exhibiting in
the show window; but Jessie would not go any

farther than to order the things enumerated and ask to have them sent over the next morning.

The girls hurried home when they had done this, for it was verging on dinner time and they did not want to miss going with Nell Stanley and the Brandons to Parkville for the radio entertainment. Mr. Norwood was at home, and Jessie flew at him a good deal like an eager Newfoundland puppy.

"It is the most wonderful thing!" she declared, as she had introduced the subject to her chum.

She kept up the radio talk all through dinner. She was so interested that for the time being she forgot all about the girl that had been carried away in the automobile. Mr. Norwood had not been much interested in the new science; but he promised to talk the matter over with Momsy after their daughter had gone to the radio concert.

"Anyhow," said Jessie, "I've bought the books telling how to rig it. And we're going to do it all ourselves—Amy and I. And Mr. Brill is going to send up some wire and things. Of course, if you won't let me have it, I'll just have to pay for the hardware out of my allowance."

"Very well," her father said with gravity. "Maybe Chapman can find some use for the hardware if we don't decide to build a radio station."

As they seldom forbade their daughter anything that was not positively harmful, however, there was not much danger that Jessie's allowance would be depleted by paying a share of the monthly hardware bill. Anyhow, Jessie as well as Amy, went off very gayly in the Brandon car with the minister's daughter. Mr. Brandon drove his own car, and the girls sat in the tonneau with Mrs. Brandon, who did not seem by any means a very old lady, even if she was a grandmother.

"But grandmothers nowadays aren't crippled up with rheumatism and otherwise decrepit," declared Amy, the gay. "You know, I think it is rather nice to be a grandmother these days. I am going to matriculate for the position just as soon as I can."

They rolled out of town, and just as they turned off the boulevard to take another road to Parkville, a big car passed the Brandon automobile coming into town. It was being driven very rapidly, but very skillfully, and the car was empty save for the driver.

"What beautiful cars those French cars are," Mrs. Brandon said.

"Did you see her, Jess?" cried Amy, excitedly. "Look at her go!"

"Do you speak of the car or the lady?" laughed Nell Stanley.

"She is no lady, I'd have you know," Amy rejoined scornfully. "Didn't you know her when she passed, Jess?"

"I thought it was the car," her chum admitted. "Are you sure that was the woman who ran off with the girl?"

"One of them," declared Amy, with confidence. "And how she can drive!"

Naturally Mrs. Brandon and Nell wished to know the particulars of the chums' adventure. But none of them knew who the strange woman who drove the French car was.

"She is not at all nice, at any rate," Jessie said emphatically. "I really wish there was some way of finding out about that girl they carried off, and what became of her."

Stringing the Aerials

CHAPTER IV

STRINGING THE AERIALS

PARKVILLE was reached within a short time. It was still early evening. The girls from Roselawn and their host and hostess found a number of neighbors already gathered in the drawing-room, to listen to the entertainments broadcasted from several radio stations.

They were too late for the bedtime story; but from the cabinet-grand, like an expensive talking machine, the slurring notes of a jazz orchestra greeted their ears as plainly as though it were coming from a neighboring room instead of a broadcasting station many miles away. Amy confessed that it made her feet itch. She loved to dance.

There was singing to follow, a really good quartette. Then a humorist told some of his own funny stories and an elocutionist recited a bit from Shakespeare effectively. The band played a popular air and the amused audience began singing the song. It was fine!

"I'm just as excited as I can be," whispered Jessie to Nell and Amy. "Isn't it better than our talking machine? Why! it is almost like hearing the real people right in the room. And an amplifier of this kind is not scratchy one bit."

"There is no static to-night," said Mr. Brandon, who overheard the enthusiastic girl. "But it is not always so clear."

Jessie and Amy were too excited over this new amusement to heed anything that suggested "a fly in the ointment." When they drove home they were so full of radio that they chattered like magpies.

"I would put up the aerials and get a set myself," Nell declared, "only we don't really need any more talking machines of any kind at our house. Dear me! I sometimes wonder how the Reverend can write his sermons, there is so much noise and talk all the time. I have tacked felt all around his study door to try to make it soundproof. But when Bob comes in he bangs the outer door until you are reminded of the Black Tom explosion. And Fred never comes downstairs save on his stomach—and on the banisters—and lands on the doormat like a load of brick out of a dumpcart. Then Sally squeals so!" She sighed.

"Nell Stanley," Amy said, "certainly has her own troubles."

"I do not see how the doctor stands it," commented Mrs. Brandon sympathetically.

"The Reverend is the greatest man in the world," declared Nell. with conviction. "He is

wonderful. He takes the most annoying things
so composedly. Why, you remember when he
went to Bridgeton a month ago to speak at the
local Sunday School Union? Something awfully
funny happened. It would have floored any man
but the Reverend."

"What happened?" asked Amy. "I bet it was
a joke. Your father, Nell, always tells the most
delightful stories."

"This isn't a story. It is so," chuckled Nell.
"But I suppose that was why they asked him to
amuse and entertain the little folks at one session
of the Union. Father talked for fifteen minutes,
all about Jacob's ladder, and those old stories.
And not a kid of 'em went to sleep.

"He said he was proud to see them so wide
awake, and when he was closing he thought he
would find out if they really had been attentive.
So he said:

" 'And now, is there any little boy or any little
girl who would like to ask me a question?'

"And one boy called out: 'Say, Mister, if the
angels had wings why did they walk up and down
Jacob's ladder?' "

"Mercy!" ejaculated Mrs. Brandon. "What
could he say?"

"That is it. You can't catch the Reverend,"
laughed Nell, proudly. "And nothing ever con-
fuses him or puts him out. He just said:

" 'Oh, ah, yes, I see. And now, is there any little boy or any little girl who would like to answer that question?' And he bowed and slipped out."

The laughter over this incident brought them into Roselawn, where Jessie and Amy got out, after thanking the kindly Brandons for the evening's pleasure. Nell lived a little further along, and went on with Mr. and Mrs. Brandon.

"If I can find the time," called Nell Stanley, as the car started again, "I am coming over to see how you rig your aerials, Jessie."

"If I am allowed to," commented Jessie, with a sudden fear that perhaps her father would find some objection to the new amusement.

But this small fear was immediately dissipated when she ran in after bidding Amy good-night. She found her father and mother both in the library. The package of radio books had been opened, and Mr. and Mrs. Norwood was each reading interestedly one of the pamphlets Jessie had chosen at the bookshop.

The three spent an hour discussing the new "plaything," as Mr. Norwood insisted upon calling it. But he agreed to everything his daughter wanted to do, and even promised to buy Jessie a better receiving set than Brill, the hardware man, was carrying.

"As far as I can see, however, from what I read

here," said Mr. Norwood, "a better set will make no difference in your plans for stringing the aerials. You and Amy can go right ahead."

"Oh, but, Robert," said Mrs. Norwood, "do you think the two girls can do that work?"

"Why not? Of course Jessie and Amy can. If they need any help they can ask one of the men —the chauffeur or the gardener, or somebody."

"We are going to do it all ourselves!" cried Jessie, eagerly. "This is going to be our very owniest own radio. You'll see. We'll put the set upstairs in my room."

"Wouldn't you rather have it downstairs—in the drawing-room, for instance?" asked her mother.

"I know you, Momsy. You'll be showing it off to all your friends. And pretty soon it will be the family radio instead of mine."

Mr. Norwood laughed. "I read here that the ordinary aerials will do very well for a small instrument or a large. It is suggested, too, that patents are pending that may make outside aerials unnecessary, anyway. Don't you mind, Momsy. If we find we want a nice, big set for our drawing-room, we'll have it in spite of Jessie. And we'll use her aerials, too."

The next day Brill sent up the things Jessie had purchased, but the girls could not begin the actual stringing of the copper wires until the morning following. Ample study of the directions for the work printed in the books Jessie had selected made the chums confident that they knew just what to do.

The windows of Jessie's room on the second floor of the Norwood house were not much more than seventy-five feet from the corner of an ornamental tower that housed the private electric plant belonging to the place. It was a tank tower, and water and light had been furnished to the entire premises from this tower before the city plants had extended their service out Bonwit Boulevard and through Roselawn.

Jessie's room had been the nursery when Jessie was little. It was now a lovely, comfortable apartment, decorated in pearl gray and pink, with willow furniture and cushions covered with lovely cretonne, an open fireplace in which real logs could be burned in the winter, and pictures of the girl's own selection.

Her books were here. And all her personal possessions, including tennis rackets, riding whip and spurs, canoe paddle, and even a bag of golf sticks, were arranged in "Jessie's room." Out of it opened her bedroom and bath. It was a big room, too, and if the radio was successful they could entertain twenty guests here if they wanted to.

"But, of course, father is getting a set with

phones, not with an amplifier like that one out at
Parkville," Jessie explained to her chum. "If we
want to use a horn afterward, we may. Now,
Amy, do you understand what there is to do?"

"Sure. We've got to get out our farmerette
costumes. You know, those we used in the school
gardens two years ago."

"Oh, fine! I never would have thought of
that," crowed Jessie.

"Leave it to your Aunt Amy. She's the wise
old bird," declared Amy. "I always did like
those overalls. If I climb a ladder I don't want
any skirt to bother me. If the ladder begins to
slip I want a chance to slide down like a man. Do
the 'Fireman, save my cheeld' act."

"You are as lucid as usual," confessed her
chum. Then she went on to explain: "I have
found rope enough in the barn for our purpose—
new rope. We will attach the end of the aerial
wires with the rope to the roof of the old tower.
It will enable us to make the far end of the aerials
higher than my window—you see?"

"Necessary point; I observe. Go ahead, Miss
Seymour."

"Please don't call me 'Miss Seymour,'" ob-
jected Jessie, frowning. "For the poor thing has
a wart on her nose."

"No use at all there. Not even as a collar-
button," declared Amy. "All right; you are *not*

Miss Seymour. And, come to think of it, I wonder if it was Miss Seymour I was thinking of last
night when I thought that woman driving the kidnapers' car looked like somebody I knew? Do
you think——?"

"Oh! That horrid woman! I don't dislike
Miss Seymour, you know, Amy, even if she does
teach English. I think she is almost handsome
beside that motor-car driver. Yes, I do."

"Wart and all?" murmured Amy.

But they were both too deeply interested in the
radio to linger long on other matters. They laid
out the work for the next morning, but did nothing practical toward erecting the wires and attend-
ant parts that day. Amy came over immediately
after breakfast, dressed in her farmerette costume, which was, in truth, a very practical suit
in which to work.

The girls even refused the help of the gardener.
He said they would be unable to raise the heavy
ladder to the tower window; and that was a fact.

"All right," said the practical Jessie, "then we
won't use the ladder."

"My! I am not tall enough to reach the things
up to you from the ground, Jess," drawled Amy.

"Silly!" laughed her friend. "I am going up
there to the top window in the tower. I can stand
on the window sill and drive in the hook, and hang
the aerial from there. See! We've got it all fixed

on the ground here. I'll haul it up with another rope. You stay down here and tie it on. You'll see."

"Well, don't fall," advised Amy. "The ground is hard."

It had been no easy matter for the two girls to construct their aerial. The wire persisted in getting twisted and they had all they could do to keep it from kinking. Then, too, they wanted to fasten the porcelain insulators just right and had to consult one of the books several times. Then there came more trouble over the lead-in wire, which should have been soldered to the aerial but was only twisted tight instead.

The girls worked all the forenoon. When one end of the aerial was attached properly to the tower, Amy ran in and upstairs to her chum's room and dropped a length of rope from one of the windows. Jessie came down from her perch and attached the house-end of the aerial to the rope. When Amy had the latter hauled up and fastened to a hook driven into the outside frame of Jessie's window, the antenna was complete.

At that (and it sounds easy, but isn't) they got it twisted and had to lower the house-end of the aerial again. While they were thus engaged, a taxicab stopped out in front. Amy, leaning from her chum's window, almost fell out in her sudden excitement.

"Oh, Jess! They've come!" she shouted.

"What do you mean?" demanded Jessie. "We were not expecting anybody, were we?"

"You weren't, but I was. I forgot to tell you," cried Amy. "They just went around Long Island and came up the East River and through Hell Gate and got a mooring at the Yacht Club, off City Island."

"Who are you talking about?" gasped her chum, wonderingly.

"Darry——"

"Darry!" ejaculated Jessie with mixed emotions. She glanced down at her overalls. She was old enough to want to look her best when Darrington Drew was on the scene. "Darry!" she murmured again.

"Yes. And Burd Alling. They telephoned early this morning. But I forgot. Here they come, Jess!"

Jessie Norwood turned rather slowly to look. She felt a strong desire to run into the house and make a quick change of costume.

The Freckle-Faced Girl

CHAPTER V

OF the two young fellows hurrying in from the boulevard one was tall and slim and dark; the other was stocky—almost plump, in fact—and sandy of complexion, with sharp, twinkling pond-blue eyes. Burdwell Alling's eyes were truly the only handsome feature he possessed. But he had a wonderfully sweet disposition.

Darry Drew was one of those quiet, gentlemanly fellows, who seem rather too sober for their years. Yet he possessed humor enough, and there certainly was no primness about him. It was he who hailed Jessie on the ground and Amy leaning out of the window above:

"I say, fellows! Have you seen a couple of young ladies around here who have just finished their junior year at the New Melford High with flying colors? We expected to find them sitting high and dry on the front porch, ready to receive company."

"Sure we did," added Burd Alling. "They have taken the highest degree in Prunes and Prisms and have been commended by their instruc-

39

tors for excellent deportment. And among all
the calicos, they are supposed to take the bun as
prudes."

Amy actually almost fell out of the window
again, and stuck out her tongue like an impudent
urchin. "A pair of smarties," she scoffed.
"Come home and fret our ears with your college
slang. How dare you!"

"I declare! Is that Miss Amy Drew?" demanded Burd, sticking a half dollar in his eye
like a monocle and apparently observing Amy for
the first time.

"It is not," said Amy sharply. "Brush by! I
don't speak to strange young men."

But Darry had come to Jessie and shaken
hands. If she flushed self-consciously, it only
improved her looks.

"Awfully glad to see you, Jess," the tall young
fellow said.

"It's nice to have you home again, Darry,"
she returned.

Amy ran down again then, in her usual harum-
scarum fashion, and the conversation became general. How had the girls finished their high-school
year? And how had the boys managed to stay a
whole year at Yale without being asked to leave
for the good of the undergraduate body?

Was the *Marigold* a real yacht, or just a row-
boat with a kicker behind? And what were the

girls doing in their present fetching costumes?

"The wires!" cried Burd. "Is it a trapeze? Are we to have a summer circus in Roselawn?"

"We shall have if you remain around here," was Amy's saucy reply. "But yon is no trapeze, I'd have you know."

"A slack wire? Who walks it—you or Jess?"

"Aw, Burd!" ejaculated Darry. "It's radio. Don't you recognize an aerial when you see it?"

"You have a fine ground connection," scoffed Burd.

"Don't you worry about us," Jessie took heart to say. "We know just what to do. Go upstairs again, Amy, and haul up this end of the contraption. I've got it untwisted."

A little later, when the aerial was secure and Jessie went practically to work affixing the ground connection, Darrington Drew said:

"Why, I believe you girls do know what you are about."

"Don't you suppose we girls know anything at all, Darry?" demanded his sister from overhead. "You boys have very little on us."

"Don't even want us to help you?" handsome Darry asked, grinning up at her.

"Not unless you approach the matter with the proper spirit," Jessie put in. "No lofty, high-and-mighty way goes with us girls. We can be met only on a plane of equality. But if you want to," she added, smiling, "you can go up to my room where Amy is and pull that rope tauter. I admit that your masculine muscles have their uses."

They were still having a lot of fun out of the securing of the aerials when suddenly Burd Alling discovered a figure planted on the gravel behind him. He swept off his cap in an elaborate bow, and cried:

"We have company! Introduce me, Amy— Jess. This young lady——"

"Smarty!" croaked a hoarse voice. "I don't want to be introducted to nobody. I want to know if you've seen Bertha."

" Big Bertha?" began Burd, who was as much determined on joking as Amy herself.

But Jessie Norwood, her attention drawn to the freckle-faced child who stood there so composedly, motioned Burd to halt. She approached and in her usual kindly manner asked what the strange child wanted.

It really was difficult to look soberly at the little thing. She might have been twelve years old, but she was so slight and undernourished looking that it was hard to believe she had reached that age. She had no more color than putty. And her sharp little face was so bespatted with freckles that one could scarcely see what its real expression was.

"Bertha who?" Jessie asked quietly. "What Bertha are you looking for?"

"Cousin Bertha. She's an orphan like me," said the freckled little girl. "I ain't got anybody that belongs to me but Bertha; and Bertha ain't got anybody that belongs to her but me."

Burd and Amy were still inclined to be amused. But Darry Drew took his cue from Jessie, if he did not find a sympathetic cord touched in his own nature by the child's speech and her forlorn appearance.

For she was forlorn. She wore no denim uniform, such as Amy had mentioned on a previous occasion as being the mark of the usual "orphan." But it was quite plain that the freckle-faced girl had nobody to care much for her, or about her.

"I wish you would explain a little more, dear," said Jessie, kindly. "Why did you come here to ask for your Cousin Bertha?"

" 'Cause I'm asking at every house along this street. I told Mrs. Foley I would, and she said I was a little fool," and the child made the statement quite as a matter of course.

"Who is Mrs. Foley?"

"She's the lady I help. When Mom died Mrs. Foley lived in the next tenement. She took me. She brought me out here to Dogtown when she moved."

"Why," breathed Amy, with a shudder, "she's one of those awful Dogtown children."

"Put a stopper on that, Amy!" exclaimed Darry, promptly.

But the freckle-faced girl heard her. She glared at the older girl—the girl so much better situated than herself. Her pale eyes snapped.

"You don't haf to touch me," she said sharply. "I won't poison you."

"Oh, Amy!" murmured her chum.

But Amy Drew was not at all bad at heart, or intentionally unkind. She flamed redly and the tears sprang to her eyes.

"Oh! I didn't mean—Forgive me, little girl! What is your name? I'll help you find your cousin."

"My name's Henrietta. They call me Hen. You needn't mind gushin' over me. I know how you feel. I'd feel just the same if I wore your clo'es and you wore mine."

"By ginger!" exclaimed Burd Alling, under his breath. "There is philosophy for you."

But Jessie felt hurt that Amy should have spoken so thoughtlessly about the strange child. She took Henrietta's grimy hand and led the freckled girl to the side steps where they could sit down.

"Now tell me about Bertha and why you are

looking for her along Bonwit Boulevard," said Jessie.

"Do you wear these pants all the time?" asked Henrietta, suddenly, smoothing Jessie's overalls. "I believe I'd like to wear 'em, too. They are something like little Billy Foley's rompers."

"I don't wear them all the time," said Jessie, patiently. "But about Bertha?"

"She's my cousin. She lived with us before Mom died. She went away to work. Something happened there where she worked. I guess I don't know what it was. But Bertha wrote to me—I can read written letters," added the child proudly. "Bertha said she was coming out to see me this week. And she didn't come."

"But why should you think——"

"Lemme tell you," said Henrietta eagerly. "That woman that hired Bertha came to Foleys day before yesterday trying to find Bertha. She said Bertha'd run away from her. But Bertha had a right to run away. Didn't she?"

"I don't know. I suppose so. Unless the woman had adopted her, or something," confessed Jessie, rather puzzled.

"Bertha wasn't no more adopted than I am. Mrs. Foley ain't adopted me. I wouldn't want to be a Foley. And if you are adopted you have to take the name of the folks you live with. So

Bertha wasn't adopted, and she had a right to run away. But she didn't get to Dogtown."

"But you think she might have come this way?"

"Yep. She's never been to see me since we moved to Dogtown. So she maybe lost her way. Or she saw that woman and was scared. I'm looking to see if anybody seen her," said the child, getting up briskly. "I guess you folks ain't, has you?"

"I am afraid not," said Jessie thoughtfully. "But we will be on the lookout for her, honey. You can come back again and ask me any time you like."

The freckle-faced child looked her over curiously. "What do you say that for?" she demanded. "You don't like me. I ain't pretty. And you're pretty—and that other girl," (she said this rather grudgingly) "even if you do wear overalls."

"Why! I want to help you," said Jessie, somewhat startled by the strange girl's downright way of speaking.

"You got a job for me up here?" asked Henrietta promptly. "I guess I'd rather work for you than for the Foleys."

"Don't the Foleys treat you kindly?" Amy ventured, really feeling an interest in the strange child.

"Guess she treats me as kind as a lady can when

she's got six kids and a man that drinks," Henrietta said with weariness. "But I'd like to wear
better clo'es. I wouldn't mind even wearing them
overall things while I worked if I had better to
wear other times."

She looked down at her faded gingham, the
patched stockings, the broken shoes. She wore
no hat. Really, she was a miserable-looking little
thing, and the four more fortunate young people
all considered this fact silently as Henrietta moved
slowly away and went down the path to the street.

"Come and see me again, Henrietta!" Jessie
called after her.

The freckled child nodded. But she did not
look around. Darry said rather soberly:

"Too bad about the kid. We ought to do
something for her."

"To begin with, a good, soapy bath," said his
sister, vigorously, but not unkindly.

"She's the limit," chuckled Burd. "Hen is some
bird, I'll say!"

"I wonder——" began Jessie, but Amy broke
in with:

"To think of her hunting up and down the
boulevard for her cousin. And she didn't even tell
us what Bertha looked like or how old she is, or
anything. My!"

"I wonder if we ought not to have asked her
for more particulars," murmured Jessie. "It is

strange we should hear of another girl that had run away——"

But the others paid no attention at the moment to what Jessie was saying· It was plain that Amy did not at all comprehend what her chum considered. The lively one had forgotten altogether about the unknown girl she and Jessie had seen borne away in the big French car.

Something Coming

CHAPTER VI

THAT afternoon Mr. Norwood brought home the radio receiving set in the automobile. The two girls, with a very little help, but a plethora of suggestion from Darry and Burd, proceeded to establish the set on a table in Jessie's room, and attach the lead-in wire and the ground wire.

Jessie had bought a galena crystal mounted, as that was more satisfactory, the book said. After all the parts of the radio set had been assembled and the connections made, the first essential operation, if they were to make use of the invention at once, was to adjust the tiny piece of wire—the "cat's whisker"—which lightly rests on the crystal-detector, to a sensitive point.

Jessie, who had read the instruction book carefully, knew that this adjustment might be made in several different ways. One satisfactory way is by the use of a miniature buzzer transmitter.

"What are we going to hear?" Amy demanded eagerly. "How you going to tune her, Jess?"

"As there are only three sets of head phones,"

grumbled Burd, "one of us is bound to be a step-child."

"We can take turns," Jessie said, eagerly. "What time is it, Darry?"

"It points to eight, Jess."

"Then there is a concert about to start at that station not more than thirty miles away from here. We ought to hear that fine," declared the hostess of the party.

"What is the wave length?" Amy asked.

"Three-sixty. We can easily get it," and Jessie adjusted the buzzer a little, the phones at her ears.

Eagerly they settled down to listen in. At least, three of them listened. Darry said he felt like the fifth wheel of an automobile—the one lashed on behind.

"I shall have to get an amplifier—a horn," Jessie murmured.

At first she heard only a funny scratchy sound; then a murmur, growing louder, as she tuned the instrument to the required wave length. The murmurous sound grew louder—more distinct. Amy squealed right out loud! For it seemed as though somebody had said in her ear:

"—and will be followed by the Sextette from Lucia. I thank you."

"We're just in time," said Burd. "They are going to begin the concert."

String music, reaching their ears so wonderfully, hushed their speech. But Darry got close to his sister, stretching his ear, too, to distinguish the sounds. The introduction to the famous composition was played brilliantly, then the voices of the singers traveled to the little group in Jessie Norwood's room from the broadcasting station thirty miles away.

"Isn't it wonderful! Wonderful!" murmured Amy.

"Sh!" admonished her chum.

When the number was ended, Burd Alling removed his head-harness and gravely shook hands with Jessie.

"Some calico, you are," he declared. "Don't ever go to college, Jess. It will spoil your initiative."

"You needn't call me by your slang terms. 'Calico,' indeed!" exclaimed Jessie. "Calico hasn't been worn since long before the war."

"You might at least call us 'ginghams,' " sniffed Amy.

"Wait!" commanded Jessie. "Here comes something else. You take my ear-tabs, Darry."

"Wait a moment," cried Amy, who still had her phones to her ears. Then she groaned horribly. "It's a lecture! Oh! Merciful Moses' aunt! Here! You listen in, Darry!"

"What's it all about?" asked her brother.

"A talk on 'The Home Beautiful,'" giggled Burd, "by One of the Victims. Come on, Darry. You may have my phones too."

As all three seemed perfectly willing to let him have their listening paraphernalia, Darry refused. "Your unanimity is poisonous," he said. "The Greeks bearing gifts."

"Let's get a rain check for this," suggested Burd.

"It will last only twenty minutes, according to the schedule," Jessie said, with a sigh. It was such a fine plaything that she disliked giving it up for a minute.

They talked, on all kinds of subjects. The boys had had no time before to tell the girls about the *Marigold*. Just such another craft it was evident had never come off the ways!

"And it is big enough to take out a party of a dozen," Darry declared. "Some time this summer we are going to get up a nice crowd and sail as far as Bar Harbor—maybe."

"Why not to the Bahamas, Darry?" drawled his sister.

"And there, too," said Darry, stoutly. "Oh, the *Marigold* is a seaworthy craft. We are going down to Atlantic Highlands in her next. Burd's got a crush on a girl who is staying there for the summer," and he said it wickedly, grinning at his sister.

"Sure," his chum agreed quickly, before Amy's tart tongue could comment. "She's my maiden aunt, and I've got a lot of things to thank her for."

"And she can't read writing, so we have to go to see her," chuckled Darry.

"Send us a snapshot of her, Darry," begged Jessie, not unwilling to tease her chum, for it was usually Amy who did the teasing.

"I should worry if Burd has a dozen maiden aunts," observed Amy scornfully, "and they all knitted him red wristlets!"

"How savage," groaned Darry. "Red wristlets, no less!"

The girls had news to relate to the boys as well. The church society was going to have a summer bazaar on the Fourth of July and a prize had been offered by the committee in charge for the most novel suggestion for a money-making "stunt" at the lawn party.

"I hope they will make enough to pay Doctor Stanley's salary," Darry said.

"We want to raise his salary," Jessie told him. "With all those children I don't see how he gets on."

"He wouldn't 'get on' at all if it wasn't for Nell," said Amy warmly. "She is a wonderful manager."

The boys departed for City Island and the

Marigold the next morning; but they promised to return from their trip to Atlantic Highlands in season for the church bazaar.

For the next few days Jessie and Amy were busy almost all day long, and evening too, with the radio. They even listened to the weather predictions and the agricultural report and market prices!

The Norwood home never had been so popular before. People, especially Jessie's school friends, were coming to the house constantly to look at the radio set and to "listen in" on the airways. The interest they all took in it was amusing.

"You see, Momsy," laughed Jessie, when she and her mother were alone one day, "if my radio set were downstairs here, I wouldn't have much use of it. Even old Mrs. Grimsby has been in twice to talk about it, and yesterday she came upstairs to try it."

"But she won't have one in her house," Mrs. Norwood said. "I don't know—I didn't think of it before, Jessie. But do you suppose it is safe?"

"Suppose what is safe, dear?"

"Having all those wires outside the house? Mrs. Grimsby says she would not risk it."

"Why not, for mercy's sake?" cried Jessie.

"Lightning. When we had a shower yesterday

I was really frightened. Those wires might draw lightning."

"But, *dear!*" gasped Jessie. "Didn't I show you the lightning switch?"

"Yes, child. I told Mrs. Grimsby about that. Do you know what she said?"

"Something funny, I suppose?"

"She said she wouldn't trust a little thing like that to turn God's lightning if He wanted to strike this house."

"O-oh!" gasped Jessie. "What a dreadful idea she must have of the Creator. "I'm going to tell Doctor Stanley that."

"I guess the good doctor has labored with Mrs. Grimsby more than once regarding her harsh doctrinal beliefs. However, the fact that such wires may draw lightning cannot be gainsaid."

"Oh, dear, me! I hope you won't worry Momsy. It can't be so, or there would be something about it in the radio papers and in those books. In one place I saw it stated that the aerials were really preventative of lightning striking the house."

"I know. They used to have lightning rods on houses, especially in the country. But it was found to be a good deal of a fallacy. I guess, after all, Mrs. Grimsby has it partly right. Human beings cannot easily command the elements which Nature controls."

"Seems to me we are disproving that right in this radio business," cried Jessie. "And it is going to be wonderful—just *wonderful*—before long. They say moving pictures will be transmitted by radio; and there will be machines so that people can speak directly back and forth, and you'll have a picture before you of the person you are speaking to."

She began to laugh again. "You know what Amy says? She says she always powders her nose before she goes to the telephone. You never know who you may have to speak to! So she is ready for the new invention."

"Just the same, I am rather timid about the lightning, Jessie," her mother said.

The Canoe Trip
Carter's Ghost

CHAPTER VII

THE CANOE TRIP

OF course, Jessie Norwood and Amy Drew did not spend all their time over the radio set in Jessie's room. At least, they did not do so after the first two or three days.

There was not much the girls cared to hear being broadcasted before late afternoon; so they soon got back to normal. Not being obliged to get off to school every day but Saturday and Sunday, had suddenly made opportunity for many new interests.

"Or, if they are not new," Amy said decisively, "we haven't worn them out."

"Do you think we shall wear out the radio, honey?" asked Jessie, laughing.

"I don't see how the air can be worn out. And the radio stuff certainly comes through the air. Or do the Hertzian waves come through the ground, as some say?"

"You will have to ask some scientist who has gone into the matter more deeply than I have," Jessie said demurely. "But what is this revived interest that you want to take up?"

"Canoe. Let's take a lunch and paddle away

down to the end of the lake. There are just
wonderful flowers there. And one of the girls
said that her brothers were over by the abandoned
Carter place and found some wild strawberries."

"M-mm! I love 'em," confessed Jessie.

"Better than George Washington sundaes,"
agreed her chum. "Say we go?"

"I'll run tell Momsy. She can play with my
radio while we are gone," and Jessie went downstairs to find her mother.

"I tell you what," said Amy as, with their paddles, the girls wended their way down to the little
boathouse and landing. "Won't it be great if they
ever get pocket radios?"

"Pocket radios!" exclaimed Jessie.

"I mean what the man said in the magazine
article we read in the first place. Don't you remember? About carrying some kind of a con-
densed receiving set in one's pocket—a receiving
and a broadcasting set, too."

"Oh! But that is a dream."

"I don't know," rejoined Amy, who had become a thorough radio convert by this time. "It
is not so far in advance, perhaps. I see one man
has invented an umbrella aerial-receiving thing—
what-you-may-call-it."

"An umbrella!" gasped Jessie.

"Honest. He opens it and points the ferrule
in the direction of the broadcasting station he is

tuned to. Then he connects the little radio set, clamps on his head harness, and listens in."

"It sounds almost impossible."

"Of course, he doesn't get the sounds very loud. But he *hears*. He can go off in his automobile and take it all with him. Or out in a boat ——Say, it would be great sport to have one in our canoe."

"You be careful how you get into it yourself and never mind the radio," cried Jessie, as Amy displayed her usual carelessness in embarking.

"I haven't got on a thing that water will hurt," declared the other girl.

"That's all right. But everything you have on can get wet. Do be still. You are like an eel!" cried Jessie.

"Don't!" rejoined Amy with a shudder. "I loathe eels. They are so squirmy. One wound right around my arm once when I was fishing down the lake, and I never have forgotten the slimy feel of it."

Jessie laughed. "We won't catch eels to-day. I never thought about fishing, anyway. I want strawberries, if there are any down there."

Lake Monenset was not a wide body of water. Burd Alling had said it was only as wide as "two hoots and a holler." Burd had spent a few weeks in the Tennessee Mountains once, and had brought back some rather queer expressions that the natives there use.

Lake Monenset was several miles long. The head of it was in Roselawn at one side of the Norwood estate and almost touched the edge of Bonwit Boulevard. It was bordered by trees for almost its entire length on both sides, and it was shaped like a enormous, elongated comma.

The gardener at the Norwood estate and his helper looked after the boathouse and the canoes. The Norwood's was not the only small estate that verged upon the lake, but like everything else about the Norwood place, its lake front was artistically adorned.

There were rose hedges down here, too, and as the two girls pushed out from the landing the breath of summer air that followed them out upon the lake was heavy with the scent of June roses.

The girls were dressed in such boating costumes as gave them the very freest movement, and they both used the paddle skillfully. The roomy canoe, if not built for great speed, certainly was built for as much comfort as could be expected in such a craft.

Jessie was in the bow and Amy at the stern. They quickly "got into step," as Amy called it, and their paddles literally plied the lake as one. Faster and faster the canoe sped on and very soon they rounded the wooded tongue of land that hid all the long length of the lower end of the lake.

"Dogtown is the only blot on the landscape," panted Amy, after a while. "It stands there right where the brook empties into the lake and—and it is unsightly. Whee!"

"What are you panting for, Amy?" demanded her chum.

"For breath, of course," rejoined Amy. "Whee! You are setting an awfully fast pace, Jess."

"I believe you are getting over-fat, Amy," declared Jessie, solemnly.

"Say not so! But I did eat an awfully big breakfast. The strawberries were so good! And the waffles!"

"Yet you insisted on bringing a great shoe box of lunch," said her friend.

"Not a *great* shoe box. Please! My own shoes came in it and I haven't enormously big feet," complained Amy. "But we must slow down."

"Just to let you admire Dogtown, I suppose?" said Jessie, laughing.

"Well, it's a sight! I wonder what became of that freckle-faced young one."

"I wonder if she found her cousin," added Jessie.

"That was a funny game; for that child to go

hunting through the neighborhood after a girl. What was her name—Bertha?"

"Yes. And I have been thinking since then, Amy, that we should have asked little Henrietta some more questions."

"Little Henrietta," murmured Amy. "How funny! She never could fill specifications for such a name."

"Never mind that," Jessie flung back over her shoulder, and still breathing easily as she set a slower stroke. "What I have been thinking about is that other girl."

"The lost girl, Bertha?"

"No, no. Or, perhaps, yes, yes!" laughed Jessie. "But I mean that girl the two women forced to go with them in the motor-car. You surely remember, Amy."

"Oh! The kidnaped girl. My! Yes, I should say I did remember her. But what has that to do with little Henrietta? And they call her 'Hen,'" she added, chuckling.

"I have been thinking that perhaps the girl Henrietta was looking for was the girl we saw being carried away by those women."

"Jess Norwood! Do you suppose so?"

"I don't know whether I suppose so or not," laughed Jessie. "But I think if I ever see that child again I shall question her more closely."

She said this without the first idea that little

Henrietta would cross their way almost at once. The canoe touched the grassy bank at the edge of the old Carter place at the far end of the lake just before noon. An end of the old house had been burned several years before, but the kitchen ell was still standing, with chimney complete. Picnic parties often used the ruin of the old house in which to sup. It was a shelter, at least.

"I've got to eat. I've got to eat!" proclaimed Amy, the moment she disembarked. "Actually, I am as hollow as Mockery."

"Well, I never!" chuckled Jessie. "Your simile is remarkably apt. And I feel that I might do justice to Alma's sandwiches, myself."

"Where's the sun gone?" suddenly demanded Amy, looking up and then turning around to look over the water.

"Why! I didn't notice those clouds. It is going to shower, Amy, my dear."

"It is going to thunder and lightning, too," and Amy looked a little disturbed. "I confess that I do not like a thunderstorm."

"Let us draw up the canoe and turn it over. Keep the inside of it dry. And we'll take the cushions up to the old house," added Jessie, briskly throwing the contents of the canoe out upon the bank.

"Ugh! I don't fancy going into the house," said Amy.

"Why not?"

"The old place is kind of spooky."

"Spooks have no teeth," chuckled Jessie. "I heard of a ghost once that seemed to haunt a country house, but after all it was only an old gentleman in a state of somnambulism who was hunting his false teeth."

"Don't make fun of spirits," Amy told her, sepulchrally.

"Why not? I never saw a ghost."

"That makes no difference. It doesn't prove there is none. How black those clouds are! O-oh! That was a sharp flash, Jessie, honey. Let's run. I guess the haunts in the old Carter house can't be as bad as standing out here in a thunder-and-lightning storm."

"To say nothing of getting our lunch wet," chuckled Jessie, following the dark girl up the grassy path with her arms filled to overflowing.

"Ah, dear me!" wailed Amy, hurrying ahead. "And those strawberries we came for. I am afraid I shall not have enough to eat without them."

The ruin of the Carter house stood upon a knoll, several great elms sheltering it. The dooryard was covered with a heavy sod and the ancient flower beds had run wild with weeds.

The place did have rather an eerie look. Most of the window panes were broken and the steps and narrow porch before the kitchen door had broken away, leaving traps for careless feet.

The thunder growled behind them. Amy quickened her steps. As she had said, she shuddered at the tempest. What might be of a disturbing nature in the old farmhouse could not, she thought, be as fearsome as the approaching tempest.

CHAPTER VIII

CARTER'S GHOST

ON the broken porch of the abandoned house Amy stopped and waited for her chum to overtake her. When she looked back she cried out again. Forked lightning blazed against the lurid clouds. It was so sharp a display of electricity that Amy shut her eyes.

Jessie, still laughing, plunged up the steps and bumped right into the sagging door. It swung inward, creakingly. Amy peered over her chum's shoulder.

"O-oh!" she crooned. "Do—do you see anything?"

"Nothing alive. Not even a rat."

"Ghosts aren't alive."

"Nothing moving, then," and Jessie proceeded to march into the rather dark kitchen. "Here's a table and some benches. You know, Miss Allister's Sunday School class picnicked here last year."

"Oh, I've been here a dozen times," confessed Amy. "But always with a crowd. You know, honey, you are no protection against ghosts."

"Don't be so ridiculous," laughed Jessie. She had put down the things she had brought up from

66

the lakeside, and now turned back to look out of the open door. "Oh, Amy! It's coming!"

There was a crash of thunder and then the rain began drumming on the roof of the porch. Jessie looked out. The clearing about the house had darkened speedily. A sheet of rain came drifting across the lake toward the hillock on which the house stood.

"Do shut the door, Jessie," begged Amy Drew.

"How ridiculous!" Jessie said again. "You can't shut the windows. There!"

Another lightning flash blinded the girls and the thunder following fairly deafened them for the moment. But Jessie did not leave her post in the doorway. Something at the edge of the clearing—some rods away, at the verge of the thick wood—had impressed itself on Jessie's sight just as the lightning flashed.

"Come away! Come away, Jess Norwood!" shrieked Amy.

"Come here," commanded Jessie. "Look. Don't be foolish. See that thing moving down there by the woods? Is it a human being or an animal?"

"Oh, Jessie! Maybe it is a ghost," murmured Amy.

But her curiosity overcame her fears sufficiently for her to join Jessie at the doorway. Through the falling rain the chums were sure that something was moving down by the woods.

"It's a dog," said Amy, after a moment.

"It's a child," declared Jessie, with conviction. "I saw its face then."

"Perhaps it *is* the Carter ghost," breathed Amy. "I never heard whether this haunt was a juvenile or an adult offender."

"I guess you are not much afraid after all," said her chum· "Yes, it is a child. And it is getting most awfully wet."

"Wait! Wait!" the girl from Roselawn cried. "Don't run away from me."

Whether the child heard and understood her or not, it gave evidence of being greatly frightened. She covered her face with her hands and sank down on the wet sod, while the rain beat upon her unmercifully. There was no shelter here, and Jessie Norwood herself was getting thoroughly wet.

In a calm moment that followed the child piped, without taking down her hands.

"Are—are you the ha'nt?"

"What a question!" gasped Jessie, and seized the crouching figure by the shoulder. "Do I feel like a ghost? Why, it's Henrietta!"

The clawlike hands dropped from the freckled face. The little girl stared.

"Goodness! I seen you before. You are the nice girl. You ain't a ghost."

"But you are sopping wet. Come up to the house at once, child."

"Ain't—ain't there ghosts there?"

"If there are they won't hurt us," said Jessie encouragingly. "Come on, child. I am getting wet myself."

But little Henrietta hung back stubbornly. "Mrs. Foley says ha'nts carry off kids. Like my Bertha was carried off."

"We have some nice lunch," said Jessie, quickly. "You'll forget all about the silly ghosts when you are helping us eat that."

This invitation and prospect overcame the fear of ghosts in Henrietta's mind. She began to trot willingly by Jessie's side. But already the rain had saturated the girl from Roselawn as well as the child from Dogtown.

"Two more bedrabbled persons I never saw!" exclaimed Amy, when they arrived upon the porch. "Do come in. There is wood here and we can make a fire on the hearth. You can take off that skirt, Jess, and get it dry. And this poor little thing—well, she looks as though she ought to be peeled to the skin if we are ever to get *her* dry."

She hustled Henrietta into the house, but kindly. She even knelt down beside her and began to unfasten the child's dress after lighting the fire that she had herself suggested. "Spooks" were evidently wiped from Amy's memory; but she flinched every time it lightened, as it did occasionally for some time.

"Say!" said the wondering Henrietta hoarsely. "I'm just as dirty as I was the other day. You don't haf to touch me."

"Oh, dear me!" cried Amy. "This child is never going to forgive me for that. Won't you like me a little, Henrietta?"

"Not as much as that other one," said the freckle-faced girl frankly.

Jessie, who was taking off her own outer garments to hang before the now roaring fire, only laughed at that.

"Tell us," she said, "why you think your cousin was carried off?"

"That lady she lived with was awful mad when she came to Foleys looking for Bertha. She said she'd put Bertha where she wouldn't run away again for one while. That's what she said."

"Oh, my dear!" exclaimed Amy suddenly. "Do you suppose—Child! did the woman come to your house——"

"Foley's house. I ain't got a house," declared Henrietta.

"Well, to Mrs. Foley's house in a big maroon automobile?" finished Amy.

"No'm. Didn't come in a car at all. She came on foot, she did. She said Bertha was a silly to run away when nothing was going to hurt her.

But she looked mad enough to hurt her," concluded the observant Henrietta.

"Oh!" exclaimed Amy again. "Was she dark
and thin and—and waspish looking?"

"Who was?" asked the child, staring.

"The woman who asked for Bertha," explained
Jessie, quite as eagerly as her chum.

"She wasn't no wasp," drawled Henrietta, with
indescribable scorn. "She was big around, like a
barrel. She was fat, and red, and ugly. I don't
like that woman. And I guess Bertha had a right
to run away from her."

Jessie and Amy looked at each other and nodded. They had both decided that the girl, Bertha,
was the one they had seen carried off in the big
French car.

"And you don't know what Bertha was afraid
of?" asked Jessie.

"I dunno. She just wrote me—I can read writing—that she was coming to see me at Foley's.
And she never come."

"Of course you did not hear anything about her
when you searched up and down the boulevard the
other day?" Amy asked.

"There wouldn't many of 'em answer questions," said the child gloomily. "Some of 'em
shooed me out of their yards before I could ask."

Amy had undressed the child now down to one
scant undergarment. She looked from her bony

little body to Jessie, and Amy's eyes actually filled with tears.

"Aren't you hungry, honey?" she asked the waif.

"Ain't I hungry?" scoffed Henrietta. "Ain't I always hungry? Mrs. Foley says I'm empty as a drum. She can't fill me up. That's how I came over here to-day."

"Because she didn't give you enough to eat?" demanded Amy, in rising wrath.

"Aw, she'd give it me if she had it. But the kids got to be fed first, ain't they? And when you've got six of 'em and a man that drinks——"

"It is quite understandable, dear," Jessie said, with more composure than her chum could display at the moment. "So you came over here——"

"To pick strawberries. Got a pail half full down there somewhere. The thunder scared me. Then I saw youse two up here and I thought you was the Carter ha'nt sure enough."

"Let's have some lunch," cried Amy quickly.

She got up and began to bustle about. She opened the two boxes they had brought and set the vacuum bottle of hot cocoa on the bench. There were two cups and she insisted upon giving one of them to Henrietta.

"I don't believe I could drink a drop or eat a morsel," she said to Jessie, when the latter remonstrated. "I feel as if I was in the famine section of Armenia or Russia or China. That poor little thing!"

She insisted upon giving Henrietta the bulk of her own lunch and all the tidbits she could find in Jessie's lunchbox. The freckle-faced girl began systematically to fill up the hollow with which she was accredited. It was evident that the good food made Henrietta quite forget the so-called ha'nts.

The rain continued to fall torrentially; the thunder muttered almost continually, but in the distance; again and again the lightning flashed.

Jessie Norwood fed the fire on the hearth until the warmth of it could be felt to the farther end of the big old kitchen. She and Henrietta were fast becoming dried, and their outer clothing could soon be put on again.

"I wonder if Momsy was scared when the storm broke," ruminated Jessie. "She thinks the aerial may attract lightning."

"Nothing like that," declared Amy cheerfully. "But I wish we had a radio sending set here and could talk to her——"

"Ow! What's that?"

Even Henrietta stopped eating, looked upward at the dusty ceiling, and listened for a repetition of the sound. It came in a moment—a sudden thump—then the thrashing about of something on the bare boards of the floor of the loft over the kitchen.

"O-oh!" squealed Amy, jumping up from the table.

"What can it be?" demanded Jessie Norwood, and her face expressed fear likewise.

Henrietta took another enormous bite of sand-wich; from behind that barrier she said in a muffled tone:

"Guess it's the Carter ha'nt after all!"

Henrietta is Valiant
The Prize Idea

CHAPTER IX

HENRIETTA IS VALIANT

JESSIE NORWOOD tried to remember that she should set little Henrietta a good example. She should not show panic because of the mysterious noise in the loft of the abandoned Carter house.

But as the thrashing sounds continued and finally the cause of it came tumbling down the enclosed stairway and bumped against the door that opened from the kitchen upon that stairway, Jessie screamed almost as loud as Amy.

Amy Drew, however, ran out into the rain. Neither Jessie nor the little freckle-faced girl were garbed properly for an appearance in the open; not even in as lonely a place as the clearing about the old Carter house. To tell the truth, Henrietta kept on eating and did not at first get up from the table.

"Aren't you scared, child?" demanded Jessie, in surprise.

"Course I am," agreed the little girl. "But ha'nts chase you anywhere. They can go right through keyholes and doors——"

"Mercy! Whatever it is seems determined to come through that door."

"There ain't no keyhole to it," said Henrietta complacently.

The banging continued at the foot of the stairs. Amy was shrieking for her chum to come out of the house. But Jessie began to be ashamed of her momentary panic.

"I'm going to see what it is," she declared, approaching the door.

"Maybe you won't see nothing," said Henrietta. "Mrs. Foley says that ha'nts is sometimes just wind. You don't see nothing. Only you feel creepy and cold fingers touch you and a chilly breath hits the back o' your neck."

"I declare!" exclaimed Jessie. "That Mrs. Foley ought not to tell you such things."

She looked about for some weapon, for the sounds behind the door panels seemed to suggest something very material. There was a long hardwood stick standing in the corner. It might have been a mop handle or something of the kind. Jessie seized it, and with more courage again walked toward the door.

Bang, bang, thump! the noise was repeated. She stretched a tentative hand toward the latch. Should she lift it? Was there something supernatural on the stairway?

She saw the door tremble from the blows delivered upon it. There was nothing spiritual about that.

"Whatever it is——"

To punctuate her observation Jessie Norwood lifted the iron latch and jerked open the door. It was dusky in the stairway and she could not see a thing. But almost instantly there tumbled out upon the kitchen floor something that brought shriek after shriek from Jessie's lips.

"Hi!" cried Henrietta. "Did it bite you?"

Jessie did not stop to answer. She seized her skirt drying before the fire and wrapped it around her bare shoulders as she ran through the outer door. She left behind her writhing all over the kitchen floor a pair of big blacksnakes.

The fighting snakes hissed and thumped about, wound about each other like a braided rope. Probably the warmth of the fire passing up the chimney had stirred the snakes up, and it was evident that they were in no pleasant frame of mind.

"What is it? Ghosts?" cried Amy Drew, standing in the rain.

"It's worse! It's snakes!" Jessie declared, looking fearfully behind her, and in at the door.

She had dropped the stick with which she had so valiantly faced the unknown. But when that unknown had become known—and Jessie had always been very much afraid of serpents—all the girl's valor seemed to have evaporated.

"Mercy!" gasped Amy. "What's going on in there? Hear that thumping, will you?"

"They are fighting, I guess," replied her chum.

"Where's Hen?"

"She's in there, too. She didn't stop eating."

At that Amy began laughing hysterically. "She can't eat the snakes, can she?" she shrieked at last. "But maybe they'll eat her. How many snakes are there, Jess?"

"Do you suppose I stopped to count them? Dozens, maybe. They came pouring out of that dark stairway——"

"Where *is* the child?" demanded Amy, who had come up upon the porch, and was now peering in through the doorway.

The sounds from inside, like the beating of a flail, continued. Amy craned her head around the door jamb to see.

"Goodness, mercy, child!" she shouted. "Look out what you are doing! You will get bitten!"

The noise of the thrashing stopped. At least, the larger part of the noise. Henrietta came to the door with the stick that Jessie had dropped in her hand.

"I fixed 'em," she said calmly. "I just hate snakes. I always kill them black ones. They ain't got no poison. And I shut the door so if there's any more upstairs they won't come down. You can come back to dinner."

"Well, you darling!" gasped Jessie.

Her chum leaned against the door jamb while peal after peal of laughter shook her. She could just put out her hands and make motions at the freckled little girl.

"She—she—she——"

"For pity's sake, Amy Drew!" exclaimed Jessie. "You'll have a fit, or something."

"She—she didn't even—stop—chewing!" Amy got out at last.

"Bless her heart! She's the bravest little thing!" Jessie declared, shakingly. "We two great, big girls should be ashamed."

"I guess you ain't so much acquainted with snakes as I am," Henrietta said, sliding onto the bench again. "But I certainly am glad it wasn't Carter's ha'nt."

"But," cried Amy, still weak from laughing, "it *was* the ghost. Of course, those snakes had a home upstairs there. Probably in the chimney. And every time anybody came here to picnic and built a fire, they got warmed up and started moving about. Thusly, the ghost stories about the Carter house."

"Your explanation is ingenious, at any rate," admitted Jessie. "Ugh! They are still writhing. Are you sure they are dead, Henrietta?"

"That's the trouble with snakes," said the child. "They don't know enough to keep still when they're dead-ed. I smashed their heads good for 'em."

But Amy could not bear to sit down to the bench again until she had taken the stick and poked the dead but still writhing snakes out of the house. The rain was diminishing now and the thunder and lightning had receded into the distance. The two older girls ate very little of the luncheon they had brought. It was with much amazement that they watched Henrietta absorb sandwiches, cake, eggs, and fruit. She did a thorough job.

"Isn't she the bravest little thing?" Jessie whispered to her chum. "Did you ever hear the like?"

"I guess that girl we saw run away with, was her cousin all right," said Amy. "How she did fight!"

At that statement Jessie was reminded of the thing that had been puzzling her for some days. She began asking questions about Bertha, how she looked, how old she was, and how she was dressed.

"She's just my cousin. She is as old as you girls, I guess, but not so awful old," Henrietta said. "I don't know what she had on her. She ain't as pretty as you girls. Guess there ain't none of our family real pretty," and Henrietta shook her head with reflection.

"What happened to her that she wanted to leave that dreadful fat woman?" asked Amy, now, as well as her chum, taking an interest in the matter.

"There wasn't a thing happened to her that I know of," said Henrietta, shaking her head again. "But by the way that lady talked it would happen to her if she got hold of Bertha again."

"How dreadful," murmured Jessie, looking at her chum.

"I don't see how we can help the girl," said Amy. "She has been shut up some place, of course. If I could just think who that skinny woman is—or who she looks like. But how she can drive a car!"

"I think we can do something," Jessie declared. "I've had my head so full of radio that I haven't thought much about this poor child's cousin and her trouble."

"What will you do?" asked Amy.

"Tell daddy. He ought to be able to advise."

"That's a fact," agreed Amy, her eyes twinkling. "He is quite a good lawyer. Of course, not so good as Mr. Wilbur Drew. But he'll do at a pinch."

CHAPTER X

THE PRIZE IDEA

WHEN the two girls paddled back up the lake after their adventure at the old Carter house, Henrietta squatted in the middle of the canoe and seemed to enjoy the trip immensely.

"I seen these sort of boats going up and down the lake, and they look pretty. Me and Charlie Foley and some of the other boys at Dogtown made a raft. But Mr. Foley busted it with an ax. He said we had no business using the coal-cellar door and Mrs. Foley's bread-mixing board. So we didn't get to go sailing," observed the freckle-faced child.

Almost everything the child said made Amy laugh. Nevertheless, like her chum, Amy felt keenly the pathos of the little girl's situation. Perhaps with Amy Drew this interest went no farther than sympathy, whereas Jessie was already, and before this incident, puzzling her mind regarding what might be done to help Henrietta and improve her situation.

The girls paddled the canoe in to a broken landing just below the scattered shacks of Dogtown, and Henrietta went ashore. It was plain that she would have enjoyed riding farther in the canoe.

"If you see us come down this way again, honey," Amy said, "run down here to the shore and we will take you aboard."

"If Mrs. Foley will let you," added Jessie.

"I dunno what Mrs. Foley will say about the strawberries. I told her I'd bring home some if she'd let me go over there. And here I come home without even the bucket."

"It is altogether too wet to pick wild strawberries," Jessie said. "I wanted some myself. But we shall have to go another day. And you can find your bucket then, Henrietta."

The chums drove their craft up the lake and in half an hour sighted the Norwood place and its roses. Everything ashore was saturated, of course. And in one place the girls saw that the storm had done some damage.

A grove of tall trees at the head of the lake and near the landing belonging to the Norwood place was a landmark that could be seen for several miles and from almost any direction on this side of Bonwit Boulevard. As the canoe swept in toward the dock Amy cried aloud:

"Look! Look, Jess! No wonder we thought that thunder was so sharp. It struck here."

"The thunder struck?" repeated Jessie, laugh-

ing. "I *am* thunderstruck, then. You mean——
Oh, Amy! That beautiful great tree!"

She saw what had first caught Amy's eye. One
of the tallest of the trees was split from near its
top almost to the foot of the trunk. The white
gash looked like a wide strip of paper pasted down
the stick of ruined timber.

"Isn't that too bad?" said Amy, staring.

But suddenly Jessie drove her paddle deep into
the water and sent the canoe in a dash to the landing. She fended off skillfully, hopped out, and
began to run.

"What is the matter, Jess?" shrieked Amy.
"You've left me to do all the work."

"Momsy!" gasped out Jessie, looking back for
an instant. "She was scared to death that the
lightning would strike the house because of the
radio aerial."

Her chum came leaping up the hill behind her,
having moored the canoe with one hitch. She
cried out:

"No danger from lightning if you shut the
switch at the set. You know that, Jessie."

"But Monsy doesn't know it," returned the
other girl, and dashed madly into the house.

She had forgotten to tell her mother of that
fact—the safety of the closed receiving switch.
She felt condemned. Suppose her mother had
been frightened by the thunder and lightning and

should pay for it with one of her long and torturing sick headaches?

"Momsy! Momsy!" she cried, bursting into the hall.

"Your mother is down town, Miss Jessie," said the quiet voice of the parlor maid. "She drove down in her own car before the storm."

"Oh! She wasn't here when the lightning struck——"

"No, Miss Jessie. And that was some thunder-clap! Cook says she'll never get over it. But I guess she will. Bill, the gardener's boy, says it struck a tree down by the water."

"So it did," Jessie rejoined with relief. "Well, I certainly am glad Momsy wasn't here. It's all right, Amy," she called through the screen doors.

"I am glad. I thought it was all wrong by the way you ran. Now let's go back and get our rugs and the rest of the junk out of the canoe. And, oh, me! Ain't I hungry!"

Jessie ignored this oft-repeated complaint, saying:

"We should have remembered about the bazaar committee meeting. Momsy would go to that. Do you know, Amy, she thinks she can get the other ladies to agree to have the lawn party out here."

"Here, in Roselawn?" asked her chum.

"Right here on our place."

"How fine!" ejaculated Amy. "But, Jessie, I wish I could think of some awfully smart idea to work in connection with the lawn party. That lovely, lovely sports coat that Letterblair has in his window has taken my eye."

"I saw it," Jessie admitted. "And the card says it goes to the girl under eighteen who suggests the best money-making scheme in unusual channels that can be used by the bazaar committee. Yes, it's lovely."

"Let's put on our thinking-caps, honey, and try for it. Only two days more."

"And if we win it, shall we divide the coat between us?"

"No, we'll cast lots for it," said Amy seriously. "It is a be-a-utiful coat!"

That evening after dinner Jessie climbed upon the arm of her father's big chair in the library, sitting there and swinging her feet just as though she were a very small child again. He hugged her up to him with one arm while he laid down the book he was reading.

"Out with it, daughter," Mr. Norwood said. "What is the desperate need for a father?"

"It is not very desperate, and really it is none of my business," began Jessie thoughtfully.

"And that does not surprise me. It will not be the first time that you have shown interest in something decidedly not your concern."

"Oh! But I am concerned about her, Daddy."

"A lady in the case, eh?"

"A girl. Like Amy and me. Oh, no! *Not* like Amy and me. But about our age."

"What is her name and what has she done?"

"Bertha. Or, perhaps it isn't Bertha. But we think so."

"Somehow, it seems to me, you have begun wrong. Who is this young person who may be Bertha but who probably is not?"

Jessie told him about the "kidnaped" girl then. But it spilled out of her mouth so rapidly and so disconnectedly that it is little wonder that Mr. Norwood, lawyer though he was, got a rather hazy idea of the incident connected with the strange girl's being captured on Dogtown Lane.

In fact, he got that girl and little, freckled Henrietta Haney rather mixed up in his mind. He found himself advising Jessie to have the child come to the house so that Momsy could see her. Momsy always knew what to do to help such unfortunates.

"And you think there can be nothing done for that other girl?" Jessie asked, rather mournfully.

"Oh! You mean the girl you saw put in the automobile and taken away? Well, we don't know her or the woman who took her, do we?"

"No-o. Though Amy says she thinks she has

seen somebody who looks like the woman driving the car before."

"Humph! You have no case," declared Mr. Norwood, in his most judicial manner. "I fear it would be thrown out of court."

"Oh, dear!"

"If your little acquaintance could describe her cousin so that we could give the description to the police—or broadcast it by radio," and Mr. Norwood laughed.

Jessie suddenly hopped down from the chair arm and began a pirouette about the room, clapping her hands as she danced.

"I've got it! I've got it!" she cried. "Radio! Oh, Daddy! you are just the nicest man. You give me such fine ideas!"

"You evidently see your way clear to a settlement of this legal matter you brought to my attention," said Mr. Norwood quite gravely.

"Nothing like that! Nothing like that!" cried Jessie. "Oh, no. But you have given me such a fine idea for winning the prize Momsy and the other ladies are offering. I've got it! I've got it!" and she danced out of the room.

Belle Ringold
The Glorious Fourth
The Bazaar.

CHAPTER XI

WHETHER Jessie Norwood actually "had it," as she proclaimed, or not, she kept very quiet about her discovery of what she believed to be a brand new idea. She did not tell Amy, even, or Momsy. That would have been against the rules of the contest.

She wrote out her suggestion for the prize idea, sealed it in an envelope, and dropped it through the slit in the locked box in the parish house, placed there for that purpose. It was not long to wait until the next evening but one.

She rode down to the church in Momsy's car, an electric runabout, and waited outside the committee room door with some of the other girls and not a few of the boys of the parish, for there had been a prize offered, too, for the boy who made the best suggestion.

"I am sure they are going to use my idea," Belle Ringold said, with a toss of her bobbed curls.

Did we introduce you to Belle? By this speech you may know she was a very confident person, not easily persuaded that her own way was not

always best. She not only had her hair bobbed in
the approved manner of that season, but her
mother was ill-advised enough to allow her to
wear long, dangling earrings, and she favored a
manner of walking (when she did not forget)
that Burd Alling called "the serpentine slink."
Belle thought she was wholly grown up.

"They couldn't throw out my idea," repeated
Belle.

"What is it, Belle, honey?" asked one of her
chums.

"She can't tell," put in Amy, who was present.
"That is one of the rules."

"Pooh!" scoffed Belle. "Guess I'll tell if I
want to. That won't invalidate my chances.
They will be only too glad to use my idea."

"Dear me," drawled Amy, laughing. "You're
just as sure as sure, aren't you?"

Miss Seymour, the girls' English teacher in
school, came to the door of the committee room
with a paper in her hand. A semblance of order
immediately fell upon the company.

"We have just now decided upon the two sug-
gestions of all those placed in the box, the two
prize ideas. And both are very good, I must say.
Chippendale Truro! Is Chip here?"

"Yes, ma'am," said Chip, who was a snub-nosed
boy whose chums declared "all his brains were in
his head."

"Chip, I think your idea is very good. You will be interested to learn what it is, girls. Chip suggests that all the waitresses and saleswomen at the lawn party wear masks—little black masks as one does at a masquerade party. That will make them stand out from the guests. And the committee are pleased with the idea. Chip gets the tennis racket in Mr. Brill's show-window."

"Cricky, Chip! how did you come to think of that?" demanded one of the boys in an undertone.

"Well, they are going to be regular road-agents, aren't they?" asked the snub-nosed boy. "They take everything you have in your pockets at those fairs. They ought to wear masks—and carry guns, too. Only I didn't dare suggest the guns."

Amid the muffled explosion of laughter following this statement, Miss Seymour began speaking again:

"The girl's prize—the sports coat at Letterblair's—goes to Jessie Norwood, on whose father's lawn the bazaar is to be held on the afternoon and evening of the Fourth of July."

At this announcement Belle Ringold actually cried out: "What's that?"

"Hush!" commanded Miss Seymour. "Jessie has suggested that a tent be erected—her father has one stored in his garage—and that her radio set be placed in the tent and re-connected. With

an amplifier the concerts broadcasted from several stations can be heard inside the tent, and
we will charge admission to the tent. Radio is a
new and novel form of amusement and, the committee thinks, will attract a large patronage.
The coat is yours, Jessie."

"Well, isn't that the meanest thing!" ejaculated
Belle Ringold.

"Did I hear you say something, Belle?" demanded Miss Seymour, in her very sternest way.

"Well, I want to say——"

"Don't say it," advised the teacher. "The de-
cisions upon the prize ideas are arbitrary. The
committee is responsible for its acts, and must
decide upon all such matters. The affair is
closed," and she went back into the committee
room and closed the door.

"Well, isn't she the mean thing!" exclaimed
one of those girls who liked to stand well with
Belle Ringold.

"I am sure your idea was as good as good could
be, Belle," Jessie said. "Only I happened to have
the radio set, and—and everything is rigged right
for my idea to work out."

"Oh, I can see that it was rigged right,"
snapped Belle. "Your mother is on the committee, and the lawn party is going to be at your
house. Oh, yes! No favoritism shown, of
course."

"Oh, cat's foot!" exclaimed Amy, linking her arm in Jessie's. "Let her splutter, Jess. We'll go to the Dainties Shop and have a George Washington sundae."

"I am afraid Belle is going to be very unpleasant about this thing," sighed Jessie, as she and her chum came out of the parish house.

"As usual," commented Amy. "Why should we care?"

"I hate to have unpleasant things happen."

"Think of the new coat," laughed Amy. "And I do think you were awfully smart to think of using your radio in that way. Lots of people, do you know, don't believe it can be so. They think it is make-believe."

"How can they, when wireless telegraphy has been known so long?"

"But, after all, this is something different," Amy said. "Hearing voices right out of the air! Well, you know, Jess, I said before, I thought it was sort of spooky."

"Ha, ha!" giggled her chum. "All the spooks you know anything about personally are blacksnakes. Don't forget that."

"And how brave that little Hen was," sighed Amy, as they sat down to the round glass table in the Dainties Shop. "I never saw such a child."

"I was trying to get daddy interested in her and in her lost cousin—if that was her cousin whom we saw carried off," Jessie returned. "Come to think of it, I didn't get very far with my story. I must talk to daddy again. But Momsy says he is much troubled over a case he has on his hands, an important case, and I suppose he hasn't time for our small affairs."

"I imagine that girl who was kidnaped doesn't think hers is a small affair," observed Amy Drew, dipping her spoon into the rich concoction that had been placed before her. "Oh, yum, yum! Isn't this good, Jess?"

"Scrumptious. By the way, who is going to pay for it?"

"Oh, my! Haven't you any money?" demanded Amy.

"We-ell, you suggested this treat."

"But you should stand it. You won the prize coat," giggled Amy.

"I never saw the like of you!" exclaimed Jessie. "And you say I am not fit to carry money, and all. Have you actually got me in here without being able to pay for this cream?"

"But haven't you any money?" cried Amy.

"Not one cent. I shall have to hurry back to the parish house and beg some of Momsy."

"And leave me here?" demanded Amy. "Never!"

"How will you fix it, then?" asked Jessie, who

was really disturbed and could not enjoy her sundae.

"Oh, don't let that nice treat go to waste, Jess."

"It does not taste nice to me if we can't pay for it."

"Don't be foolish. Leave it to me," said Amy, getting on her feet. "I'll speak to the clerk. He's nice looking and wears his hair slicked back like patent leather. Lo-o-vely hair."

"Amy Drew! Behave!"

"I am. I am behaving right up, I tell you. I am sure I can make that clerk chalk the amount down until we come in again."

"I would be shamed to death," Jessie declared, her face flushing almost angrily, for sometimes Amy did try her. "I will not hear of your doing that. You sit down here and wait till I run back to the church———"

"Oh, you won't have to," interrupted Amy. "Here come some of the girls. We can bor-row———"

But the girl who headed the little group just then entering the door of the Dainties Shop was Belle Ringold. The three who followed Belle were her particular friends. Jessie did not feel that she wanted to borrow money of Belle or her friends.

CHAPTER XII

THE GLORIOUS FOURTH

"NEVER mind," whispered Amy Drew quickly, quite understanding her chum's feelings regarding Belle and her group. "I'll ask them. It's my fault, anyway. And I only meant it for a joke——"

"A pretty poor joke, Amy," Jessie said, with some sharpness. "And I don't want you to borrow of them. I'll run back to the church."

She started to leave the Dainties Shop. Sally Moon, who was just behind Belle Ringold, halted Jessie with a firm grasp on her sleeve.

"Don't run away just because we came in, Jess," she said.

"I'm coming right back," Jessie Norwood explained. "Don't keep me."

"Where you going, Jess?" drawled another of the group.

"I've got to run back to the church to speak to mother for a moment."

"Your mother's not there," broke in Belle. "She was leaving in her flivver when we came away. The committee's broken up and the parish house door is locked."

"Oh, no!" murmured Jessie, a good deal appalled.

"Don't I tell you *yes?*" snapped Belle. "Don't you believe me?"

"Of course I believe what you say, Belle," Jessie rejoined politely. "I only said 'Oh, no!' because I was startled."

"What scared you?" demanded Belle, curiously.

"Why, I—I'm not scared——"

"It is none of your business, Belle Ringold," put in Amy. "Don't annoy her. Here, Jessie, I'll——"

The clerk who waited on them had come to the table and placed a punched ticket for the sundaes on it. He evidently expected to be paid by the two girls. The other four were noisily grouping themselves about another table. Belle Ringold said:

"Give Nick your orders, girls. This is on me. I want a banana royal, Nick. Hurry up."

The young fellow with the "patent leather" hair still lingered by the table where Jessie and Amy had sat. Belle turned around to stare at the two guilty-looking chums. She sneered.

"What's the matter with you and Jess, Amy Drew? Were you trying to slip out without paying Nick? I shouldn't wonder!"

"Oh!" gasped Jessie, flushing and then paling.

But Amy burst out laughing. It was a fact that Amy Drew often saw humor where her chum

could not spy anything in the least laughable.
With the clerk waiting and these four girls, more
than a little unfriendly, ready to make unkind
remarks if they but knew the truth——

What should she do? Jessie looked around
wildly. Amy clung to a chair and laughed, and
laughed. Her chum desired greatly to have the
floor of the New Melford Dainties Shop open at
her feet and swallow her!

"What's the matter with you, Amy Drew?
You crazy?" demanded Belle.

"I—I——" Amy could get no farther. She
weaved back and forth, utterly hysterical.

"If you young ladies will pay me, please,"
stammered the clerk, wondering. "I'd like to wait
on these other customers."

"I want my banana royal, Nick," cried Belle.

The other three girls gave their orders. The
clerk looked from the laughing Amy to the trem-
bling Jessie. He was about to reiterate his demand for payment.

And just then Heaven sent an angel! Two, in
very truth! At least, so it seemed to Jessie
Norwood.

"Darry!" she almost squealed. "And Burd
Alling! We—we thought you were at Atlantic
Highlands."

The two young fellows came hurrying into the
shop. They had evidently seen the girls from out-

side. Darry grabbed his sister and sat her down at a table. He grinned widely, bowing to Belle and her crowd.

"Come on, Jessie!" he commanded. "No matter how many George Washington sundaes you kids have eaten——"

"'Kids'! Indeed! I like that!" exploded Amy.

But her brother swept on, ignoring her objection: "No matter how many you have eaten, there is always room for one more. You and Amy, Jessie, must have another sundae on me."

"Darry!" exclaimed Jessie Norwood. "I thought you and Burd went to his aunt's."

"And we came back. That is an awful place. There's an uncle, too—a second crop uncle. And both uncle and auntie are vegetarians, or something. Maybe it's their religion. Anyway, they eat like horses—oats, and barley, and chopped straw. We were there for two meals. Shall we ever catch up on our regular rations, Burd?"

"I've my doubts," said his friend. "Say, Nick, bring me a plate of the fillingest thing there is on your bill of fare."

"In just a minute," replied the clerk, hopping around the other table to have Belle Ringold and her friends repeat their orders.

Belle had immediately begun preening when Darry and Burd came in. That the two college youths were so much older, and that they merely considered Amy and Jessie "kids," made no difference to Belle. She really thought that she was quite grown up and that college men should be interested in her.

"We had just finished, boys," Jessie managed to say in a low tone. "We had not even paid for our sundaes."

Darry and Burd just then caught sight of the punched check lying on the table and they both reached for it. There was some little rivalry over who should pay the score, but Darry won.

"Leave it to me," he said cheerfully. "Girls shouldn't be trusted with money anyway."

"Oh! Oh!" gurgled Amy, choked with laughter again.

"What's the matter with you, Sis?" demanded her brother.

Jessie forbade her chum to tell, by a hard stare and a determined shake of her head. It was all right to have Darry pay the check—it was really a relief—but it did not seem to Jessie as though she could endure having the matter made an open joke of.

The four settled about the little table. But the Ringold crowd was too near. Belle turned sideways in her chair, even before they were served, and, being at Darry's elbow, insisted upon talking to him.

"Talk about my aunt!" said Burd Alling, grinning. "I'll tell the world that somebody has a crush on Sir Galahad that's as plain to be seen as a wart on the nose of Venus."

"Of all the metaphors!" exclaimed Amy.

Jessie feared that Belle would overhear the comments of Burd and her chum, and she hurried the eating of her second sundae.

"I must get home, Darry," she explained. "Momsy has gone without me in her car and will be surprised not to find me there."

"Sure," agreed Burd quickly. "We'll gobble and hobble. Can't you tear yourself away, Darry?" he added, with a wicked grin.

Amy's brother tried politely to turn away from Belle. But the latter caught him by the coat sleeve and held on while she chattered like a magpie to the young college man. She smiled and shook her bobbed curls and altogether acted in a rather ridiculous way.

Darry looked foolish, then annoyed. His sister was in an ecstasy of delight. She enjoyed her big brother's annoyance. She and Jessie and Burd had finished their cream.

"Come on, Darry," Burd drawled, taking a hint from the girls. "Sorry you are off your feed and can't finish George Washington's finest product. I'll eat it for you, if you say so, and then we'll beat it."

He reached casually for Darry's plate; but the latter would not yield it without a struggle. The incident, however, gave Darry a chance to break away from the insistent Belle. The latter stared at the two girls at Darry's table, sniffed, and tossed her head.

"Yes, Mr. Drew," she said in her high-pitched voice, "I suppose you have to take the children home in good season, or they would be chastised."

"Ouch!" exclaimed Burd. "I bet that hurt you, Amy."

Darry had picked up both checks from the table. Belle smiled up at him and moved her check to the edge of her table as Darry rather grimly bade her good-night. He refused to see that check, but strode over to the desk to pay the others.

"That girl ought to get a job at a broadcasting station," growled out Darry, as they went out upon the street. "I never knew before she was such a chatterbox. Don't need any radio rigging at all where she is."

"Oh, wouldn't it be fun to get a chance to work at a broadcasting station?" Amy cried. "We could sing, Jess. You know we sing well together. 'The Dartmoor Boy' and 'Bobolink, Bobolink, Spink-spank-spink' and——"

"And 'My Old Kentucky Blues,'" broke in Burd Alling. "If you are going to broadcast anything like that, give us something up to date."

"You hush," Amy said. "If Jess and I ever get the chance we shall be an honor to the program. You'll see."

That the two young fellows had returned so much earlier than had been expected was a very fortunate thing, Jessie and Amy thought. For their assistance was positively needed in the work of making ready for the Fourth of July bazaar on the Norwood place, they declared.

There were only three days in which to do everything. "And believe me," groaned Burd before the first day was ended, "we're doing everything. Talk about being in training for the scrub team!"

"It will do you good, Burdie," cooed Amy, knowing that the diminutive of Burd Alling's name would fret him. "You are getting awfully plump, you know you are."

"I feel it peeling off," he grumbled. "Don't fear. No fellow will ever get too fat around you two girls. Never were two such young Simon Legrees before since the world began!"

But the four accomplished wonders. Of course the committee and their assistants and some of the other young people came to help with the decorations. But the two girls and Amy's older brother and his friend set up the marquees and strung the Japanese lanterns, in each of which was a tiny electric light.

"No candle-power fire-traps for us," Jessie said. "And then, candles are always blowing out."

About all the relaxation they had during the time until the eve of the Fourth was in Jessie's room, listening to the radio concerts. Mr. Norwood brought out from the city a two-step amplifier and a horn and they were attached to the instrument.

The third of the month, with the help of the men servants on the Norwood place, the tent for the radio concert was set up between the house and the driveway, and chairs were brought from the parish house to seat a hundred people. It was a good tent, and there were hangings which had been used in some church entertainment in the past to help make it sound proof.

They strung through it a few electric bulbs, which would give light enough. And the lead wire from the aerials, well grounded, was brought directly in from overhead and connected with the radio set.

"I hope that people will patronize the tent generously," Jessie said. "We can give a show every hour while the crowd is here."

"What are you going to charge for admission?" Amy asked.

"Momsy says we ought to get a quarter. But ten cents——"

"Ten cents for children, grown folks a quarter," suggested Amy. "The kids will keep coming back, but the grown folks will come only once."

"That is an idea," agreed Jessie. "But what bothers me is the fact that there are only concerts at certain times. We ought to begin giving the shows early in the afternoon. Of course, the radio is just as wonderful when it brings weather reports and agricultural prices as when Toscanini sings or Volburg plays the violin," and she laughed. "But——"

"I've got it!" cried her chum, with sudden animation. "Give lectures."

"What! You, Amy Drew, suggesting such a horrid thing? And who will give the lecture?"

"Oh, this is a different sort of lecture. Tell a little story about the radio, what has already been done with it, and what is expected of it in the future. I believe you could do it nicely, Jess. That sort of lecture I would stand for myself."

"I suppose somebody has got to attend to the radio and talk about it. I had not thought of that," agreed Jessie. "I'll see what the committee say. But me lecture? I never did think of doing that!" she proclaimed, in no little anxiety.

CHAPTER XIII

THE BAZAAR

WHEN she had talked it over with Momsy and Miss Seymour, however, Jessie Norwood took up the thought of the radio lecture quite seriously. Somebody must explain and manage the entertainment in the radio tent, and who better than Jessie?

"It is quite wonderful how much you young people have learned about radio—so much more than I had any idea," said the school teacher. "Of course you can write a little prose essay, Jessie, get it by heart, and repeat it at each session in the tent, if you feel timid about giving an off-hand talk on the subject."

"You can do it if you only think you can, Jessie," said her mother, smiling. "I am sure I have a very smart daughter."

"Oh, now, Momsy! If they should laugh at me——"

"Don't give them a chance to laugh, dear. Make your talk so interesting and informative that they can't laugh."

Thus encouraged, Jessie spent all the forenoon

of the Fourth shut up in her own room making ready for the afternoon and evening. She had already made a careful schedule of the broadcasting done by all the stations within reach of her fine radio set, and found that it was possible, by tuning her instrument to the wave lengths of different stations, to get something interesting into every hour from two o'clock on until eleven.

Naturally, some of the entertainments would be more interesting or amusing than others; but as New Melford people for the most part were as yet unfamiliar with radio, almost anything out of the air would seem curious and entertaining.

"Besides," Burd Alling said in comment on this, "for a good cause we are all ready and willing to be bunkoed a little."

"Let me tell you, Mr. Smarty," said Amy, "that Jessie's lecture is well worth the price of admission alone. Never mind the radio entertainment."

"I'll come to hear it every time," agreed Burd. "You can't scare me!"

The radio had been carefully tried out in the tent the evening before. The boys had got the market reports and the early baseball scores out of the air on Fourth of July morning, before the bazaar opened. When Jessie came out after luncheon to take charge of the radio tent, she felt that she was letter perfect in the "talk" she had arranged to introduce each session of the wireless entertainment.

No admission was charged to the Norwood grounds; but several of the older boys had been instructed to keep an oversight of the entire place that careless and possibly rough youngsters should do no harm. The Norwoods', like the Drews' was one of the show places of the Roselawn section of New Melford. Boys and girls might do considerable harm around the place if they were not under discipline.

The girls and boys belonging to the congregation of Dr. Stanley's church were on hand as flower sellers, booth attendants, and waitresses. Ice-creams and sherbets were served from the garage; sandwiches and cake from the house kitchen, where Mrs. Norwood's cook herself presided proudly over the goodies.

In several booths were orangeade, lemonade, and other soft drinks. The fancy costumes and the funny masks the girls and boys wore certainly were "fetching." That the masks were the result of a joke on Chip Truro's part made them none the less effective.

Amy was flying about, as busy as a bee. Darry and Burd were at the head of the "police." Miss Seymour took tickets for the radio tent, and after the first entertainment, beginning at two o'clock, she complimented Jessie warmly on the success of her talk on radio with which the girl introduced the show.

The lawns of the Norwood place began to be crowded before two o'clock. Cars were parked for several blocks in both directions. Special policemen had been sent out from town to patrol the vicinity. Dr. Stanley's smile, as he walked about welcoming the guests, expanded to an almost unbelievable breadth.

The noisy and explosive Fourth as it used to be is now scarcely known. Our forefathers did not realize that freedom could be celebrated without guns and firecrackers and the more or less smelly and dangerous burning of powder.

"Now," stated Burd Alling pompously, "we celebrate the name of the Father of his Country with a dish of fruit ice-cream. How are the mighty fallen! A George Washington sundae, please, with plenty of 'sundae' on it. Thank you!"

Then he gave up twice the price that he would have had to pay at the Dainties Shop down town for the same concoction to the young lady in the Columbine skirt and the mask.

"Young Truro had it right," grumbled Darry. "It's a hold-up."

"But you know you like to be robbed for a good cause," chuckled Amy, who chanced to hear these comments. "And remember that Doctor Stanley is going to get his share out of this."

"Right-o," agreed Burd. "The doctor is all right."

"But we ought to pony up the money for his support like good sports," said Darry, continuing to growl.

"You'd better ask him about that," cried Amy. "Do you know what the dear doctor says? He is glad, he says, to know that so many people who never would by any chance come to hear him preach give something to the support of the church. They are in touch with the church and with him on an occasion like this, when by no other means could they be made to interest themselves in our church save to look at the clock face in the tower as they go past."

"Guess he's right there," said Burd. "I reckon there are some men on the boulevard whose only religious act is to set their watches by the church clock as they ride by to town in their automobiles."

However and whatever (to quote Amy again), the intentions were that brought the crowd, the Norwood place was comfortably filled. The goodies were bought, the sale of fancy goods added much to the treasury, and a bigger thing than any other source of income was the admission to the radio shows.

The children were not the most interested part of the audience in the tent. From two o'clock until closing time Jessie Norwood presided at eight shows. She sometimes faced almost the same audience twice. Not only did some of the children pay their way in more than once, but grown people did the same. Curiosity regarding radio science was rife.

Doctor Stanley came more than once himself to listen. And the minister's boys wanted to take the radio set all apart between shows to "see how it went."

"I bet we could build one our own selves," declared Bob Stanley.

"I betcha!" agreed Fred.

"Only, it will cost a lot of money," groaned the minister's oldest son.

"You can do it for about ten dollars—if you are ingenious," said Jessie encouragingly.

"Gee whiz! That's a lot of money," said Fred.

The girl knew better than to suggest lending them or giving them the money. But she told them all the helpful things she could about setting up the radio paraphernalia and rigging the wires.

"I guess Nell would help us," Bob remarked. "She's pretty good, you know, for a girl."

"I like that!" exclaimed Jessie.

Bob Stanley grinned at her impishly.

In the evening when the electric lights were ablaze the Norwood lawns were a pretty sight indeed. People came in cars from miles away. It was surprising how many came, it seemed, for the purpose of listening to the radio. That feature had been well advertised, and it came at a time when the popular curiosity was afire through reading so much about radio in the newspapers.

Among the hundreds of cars parked near by were those of several of the more prosperous farmers of the county. One ancient, baldheaded, bewhiskered agriculturist sat through three of the radio shows, and commented freely upon this new wonder of the world.

"The telegraph was just in its infancy when I was born," he told Jessie. "And then came the telephone, and these here automobiles, and flying machines, and wireless telegraph, and now this. Why, ma'am, this radio beats the world! It does, plumb, for sure!"

The surprise and the comments of the audience did not so much interest Jessie Norwood as the fact that the money taken in by the tent show would add vastly to the profit of the bazaar.

"You sure have beaten any other individual concession on the lot," Amy told her at the end of the evening. "You know, Belle Ringold bragged that she was going to take in the most money at the orangeade stand, because it was a hot night. But wait till we count up! I am sure you have beaten her with the radio tent, Jess."

Jealousy
Can it Be Possible?

CHAPTER XIV

JEALOUSY

JESSIE NORWOOD had not much personal desire to "beat" either Belle Ringold or any other worker for the bazaar; but she confessed to a hope that the radio show had helped largely to make up the deficit in church income for which the bazaar had been intended.

Miss Seymour had added up after each show the amount taken in at the door of the tent. Before the lights were put out and the booths were dismantled she was ready to announce to the committee the sum total of the radio tent's earnings.

"Goody! That will beat Belle, sure as you live," Amy cried when she heard it, and dragged Jessie away across the lawn to hear the report of the sum taken from the cash-drawer under the organeade counter. Groups of young people milled around the "concession" which served the delicious cooling drinks.

"Walk right up, ladies and gentlemen—and anybody else that's with you—and buy the last of the chilled nectar served by these masked goddesses. In other words, buy us out so we can all go home." It was Darry Drew up on a stool ballyhooing for the soft drink booth.

"Did you ever?" gasped the young collegian's sister. "He is helping that Belle Ringold. I am amazed at Darry!"

"He is helping the church society," said Jessie, composedly.

But she could easily believe that Belle had deliberately entangled Darry in this thing. He never would have chosen to help Belle in closing out her supply of orangeade.

There she stood behind her counter, scarcely helping wait on the trade herself, but aided by three of her most intimate girl friends. Belle gave her attention to Darry Drew. She seemed to consider it necessary to steady him upon the stool while he acted as "barker."

"Come away, do!" sniffed Amy to Jessie. "That brother of mine is as weak as water. Any girl, if she wants to, can wind him right around her finger."

But Jessie did not wholly believe that. She knew Darry's character pretty well, perhaps better than Amy did. He would be altogether too easygoing to refuse to help Belle, especially in a good cause. Belle Ringold was very shrewd, young as she was, in the arts of gaining and holding the attention of young men.

But Darry saw his sister coming and knew that

Amy disapproved. He flushed and jumped down from the stool.

"Oh, Mr. Drew! Darrington!" cried Belle, languishingly, "you won't leave us?" Then she, too, saw Amy and Jessie approaching. "Oh, well," Belle sneered, "if the children need you, I suppose you have to go."

Burd, who stood by, developed a spasm of laughter when he saw Amy's expression of countenance, but Jessie got her chum away before there came any further explosion.

"Never you mind!" muttered Amy. "I know you've got her beaten with your radio show. You see!"

It proved to be true—this prophecy of Amy's. The committee, adding up the intake of the various booths, reported that the radio tent had been by far the most profitable of any of the various money-making schemes. By that time the booths were entirely dismantled and almost everybody had gone home.

Belle and her friends had lingered on the Norwood veranda, however, to hear the report. It seemed that Belle had not achieved all that she had desired, although with the restaurant department, her stand had won a splendid profit. Of course, the money taken in at the radio tent was almost all profit.

"She just thought of that wireless thing so as

to make the rest of us look cheap," Belle was heard to say to her friends. "Isn't that always the way when we come up here to the Norwoods'? Jess skims the cream of everything. I'll never break my back working for a church entertainment again if the Norwoods have anything to do with it!"

Unfortunately Jessie heard this. It really spoiled the satisfaction she had taken in the fact that her idea, and her radio set, had made much money for a good cause. She stole away from her chum and the other young people and went rather tearfully to bed.

Of course, she should not have minded so keenly the foolish talk of an impertinent and unkind girl. But she could not help wondering if other people felt as Belle said she felt about the Norwoods. Jessie had really thought that she and Daddy and Momsy were very popular people, and she had innocently congratulated herself upon that fact.

The morning brought to Jessie Norwood more contentment. When Momsy told her how the ladies of the bazaar committee had praised Jessie's thoughtfulness and ingenuity in supplying the radio entertainment, she forgot Belle Ringold's jealousy and went cheerfully to work to help clear up the grounds and the house. Her radio set was moved back to her room and she restrung the wires and connected up the receiver without help from anybody.

When Mr. Norwood came home that evening both she and Momsy noticed at once that he was grave and apparently much troubled. Perhaps, if their thought had not been given so entirely to the bazaar during the last few days, the lawyer's wife and daughter would before this have noticed his worriment of mind.

"Is it that Ellison case, Robert?" Mrs. Norwood asked, at the dinner table.

"It is the bane of my existence," declared the lawyer, with exasperation. "Those women are determined to obtain a much greater share of the estate than belongs to them or than the testator ever intended. Their testimony, I believe, is false. But as the apportionment of the property of the deceased Mr. Ellison must be decided by verbal rather than written evidence, the story those women tell—and stick to—bears weight with the Surrogate."

"Your clients are likely to lose their share, then?" his wife asked.

"Unless we can get at the truth. I fear that neither of those women knows what the truth means. Ha! If we could find the one witness, the one who was present when the old man dictated his will at the last! Well!"

"Can't you find her?" asked Momsy, who had,

it seemed, known something about the puzzling case before.

"Not a trace. The old man, Abel Ellison, died suddenly in Martha Poole's house. She and the other woman are cousins and were distantly related to Ellison. He had a shock or a stroke, or something, while he was calling on Mrs. Poole. It did not affect his brain at all. The physicians are sure of that. Their testimony is clear.

"But neither of them heard what the old man said to the lawyer that Mrs. Poole sent for. Mc-Cracken is a scaly practitioner. He has been bought over, body and soul, by the two women. You see, they are a sporty crowd—race track habitues, and all that. The other woman—her name is Bothwell—has driven automobiles in races. She is a regular speed fiend, they tell me.

"Anyhow, they are all of a kind, the two women and McCracken. As Ellison had never made a will that anybody knows of, and this affidavit regarding his dictated wishes is the only instrument brought into court, the Surrogate is inclined to give the thing weight.

"Here comes in our missing witness, a young girl who worked for Mrs. Poole. She was examined by my chief clerk and admitted she heard all that was said in the room where Ellison died. Her testimony diametrically opposes several

items which McCracken has written into the un-
signed testament of the deceased.

"You see what we are up against when I tell
you that the young girl has disappeared. Martha
Poole says she has run away and that she does
not know where she went to. The girl seems
to have no relatives or friends. But I have my
doubts about her having run away. I think she
has been hidden away in some place by the two
women or by the lawyer."

"Oh, Daddy!" exclaimed Jessie, who had been
listening with interest. "That is just like the girl
I tried to tell you about the other night—little
Henrietta's cousin. *She* was carried off by two
women in an automobile. What do you think,
Daddy? Could Bertha be the girl you are looking for?"

CHAPTER XV

CAN IT BE POSSIBLE?

"WHAT is this?" Mr. Norwood asked, staring at his eager daughter. "Have I heard anything before about a girl being carried away?"

"Why, don't you remember, Daddy, about Henrietta who lives over in Dogtown, and her cousin, Bertha, and how Bertha has disappeared, and—and——"

"And Henrietta is the champion snake killer of all this region?" chuckled Mr. Norwood. "I certainly have a vivid remembrance of the snakes, at any rate."

"Dear me!" cried Momsy. "This is all new to me. Where are the snakes, Jessie?"

"Gone to that bourne where both good and bad snakes go," rejoined her husband. "Come, Jessie! It is evident I did not get all that you wanted to tell me the other evening. And, it seems to me, if I remember rightly, you got so excited over your radio business before you were through that you quite forgot the snakes—I mean forgot the girl you say was run away with."

"Don't joke her any more, Robert," advised Momsy. "I can see she is in earnest."

"You just listen here, Daddy Norwood," Jessie cried. "Perhaps you'll be glad to hear about Bertha. She is little Henrietta Haney's cousin, and Henrietta expected Bertha to come to see her where she lives with the Foleys in Dogtown.

"Well, the day that Bertha was expected, she didn't come. That was the day Amy and I first thought of building our radio. And when we were walking into town we heard a girl screaming in Dogtown Lane. So we ran in, and there was this girl being pulled into an automobile by two women."

"What girl was this?" asked Mr. Norwood, quite in earnest now. "A girl you and Amy knew?"

"We had never seen her before, Daddy. And I am not positive, of course, that she was Bertha, Henrietta's cousin. But Amy and I thought it might be. And now you tell about two women who want to keep a servant girl away from you, and it might be the same."

"It might indeed," admitted Mr. Norwood thoughtfully. "Tell me what the two women looked like. Describe them as well as you can."

Jessie did so. She managed, even after this length of time, to remember many peculiarities about the woman who drove the big car and the fleshy one who had treated the girl so roughly. Mr. Norwood exclaimed at last:

"I should not be at all surprised if that were Martha Poole and Mrs. Bothwell. The descriptions in a general way fit them. And if it is so, the girl Jessie and Amy saw abused in that way is surely the maid who worked for Mrs. Poole."

"Oh, Robert! can it be possible, do you think?" cried his wife.

"Not alone possible, but probable," declared Robert Norwood. "Jessie, I am glad that you are so observant. I want you to get the little girl from Dogtown some day soon and let me talk with her. Perhaps she can tell me something about her cousin's looks that will clinch the matter. At least, she can tell us her cousin's full name, I have no doubt."

"It's Bertha for a first name," said Jessie, eagerly. "And I supposed it was Haney, like Henrietta's."

"The girl I am looking for is not named Haney, whatever her first name may be. Anyway, it is a chance, and I mean to get to the bottom of this mysterious kidnaping if I can, Jessie. Let me see this little Henrietta who kills snakes with such admirable vigor," and he laughed.

It was, however, no inconsiderable matter, as Jessie well understood. In the morning she hurried over to the Drew house to tell Amy about

it. Both had been interested from the very beginning in the mystery of the strange girl and her two
women captors. There was something wrong
with those women. Amy said this with a serious
shake of her head. You could tell!

And when, on further discussion, Jessie remembered their names—Poole and Bothwell—this
fact brought out another discovery.

"Bothwell! I never did!" ejaculated Amy
Drew. "Why, no wonder I thought she looked
like somebody I knew. And she drives a fast
car—I'll say she does. Jess Norwood! where
were our wits? Don't you remember reading
about Sadie Bothwell, whose husband was one of
the first automobile builders, and she has driven
in professional races, and won a prize—a cup, or
something? And her picture was in the paper."

"That is the person Daddy refers to," Jessie
agreed. "I did not like her at all."

"Ho! I should say not!" scoffed Amy. "And
I wasn't in love with the fat woman. So she is
a race track follower, is she?" Then Amy giggled. "I guess she wouldn't follow 'em far afoot!
She isn't so lively in moving about."

"But where do you suppose they took Bertha—
if it was Henrietta's cousin we saw carried off?"

"Now, dear child, I am neither a seventh
daughter of a seventh daughter nor——"

"Nor one of the Seven Sleepers," laughed Jessie. "So you cannot prophesy, can you? We will go down to Dogtown this afternoon and see if Mrs. Foley will let us bring Henrietta back to see Daddy."

"The child hasn't been up to see you at all, has she?" asked Amy.

"Why, no."

"Maybe the woman won't want her to come. Afraid somebody may take little Hen away from her. Did you see the child's hands? They have been well used to hard work. I have an idea she is a regular little slave."

"Oh, I hope not. It doesn't seem to me as though anybody could treat that child cruelly. And she doesn't seem to blame Mrs. Foley for her condition."

"Well, Hen knows how to kill snakes, but maybe she is a poor judge of character," laughed Amy. "I'll go with you and defend you if the Foley tribe attack in force. But let's go down in the canoe. Then we can steal the cheeld, if necessary. 'Once aboard the lugger!' you know, 'and the gal is mine'."

"To hear you, one would think you were a real pirate," scoffed Jessie.

At lunch time Nell Stanley had an errand in the neighborhood, and she dropped in at the Drew house. The three girls, Mrs. Drew being away, had a gay little meal together, waited on by the

Drew butler, McTavish, who was a very grave
and solemn man.

"Almost ecclesiastic, I'll say," chuckled Nell,
when the old serving man was out of the room.
"He is a lot more ministerial looking than the
Reverend. I expect him, almost any time, to say
grace before meat. Fred convulsed us all at the
table last evening. We take turns, you know,
giving thanks. And at dinner last evening it was
the Reverend's turn.

" 'Say, Papa,' Fred asked afterward—he's
such a solemn little tike you have no idea what's
coming—'Say, Papa, why is it you say a so-much
longer prayer than I do?'

" 'Because you're not old enough to say a long
one,' Reverend told him.

" 'Oh!' said Master Freddie, 'I thought maybe it was 'cause I wasn't big enough to be as wicked
as you and I didn't need so long a one.' Now!
What can you do with a young one like that?"
she added, as the girls went off into a gale of
laughter.

But she had other news of her young brothers besides this. Bob and Fred were enamored
of the radio. They were ingenious lads. Nell
said she believed they could rig a radio set with a
hair-pin and a mouse-trap. But she was going to
help them obtain a fairly good set; only, because
of the shortage of funds at the parsonage, Bob

and Fred would be obliged themselves to make every part that was possible.

So she drew from Jessie and from Amy all they knew about the new science, and Jessie ran across to her house and got the books she had bought dealing with radio and the installation of a set.

Jessie and Amy got into their outing clothes when Nell Stanley had gone and embarked upon the lake, paddling to the landing at despised Dogtown. It was not a savory place in appearance, even from the water-side. As the canoe drew near the girls saw a wild mob of children, both boys and girls, racing toward the broken landing.

"Why! What are they ever doing?" asked Jessie, in amazement, backing with her paddle.

"Chasing that young one ahead," said Amy.

They were all dressed most fantastically, and the child running in advance, an agile and bedrabbled looking little creature, was more in masquerade than the others. She wore an old poke bonnet and carried a crooked stick, and there seemed to be a hump upon her back.

"Spotted Snake! Spotted Snake! Miss Spotted Snake!" the girls from Roselawn heard the children shrieking, and without doubt this opprobrious epithet referred to the one pursued.

Spotted Snake, The Witch
Broadcasting

CHAPTER XVI

SPOTTED SNAKE, THE WITCH

"WHAT are they trying to do to that poor child?" repeated Jessie Norwood, as the crowd swept down to the shore.

"Spotted snake! Spotted Snake!" yelled the crowd, and spread out to keep the pursued from running back. The hump-backed little figure with poke-bonnet and cane was chased out upon the broken landing.

"She will go overboard!" shrieked Jessie, and drove in her paddle again to reach the wharf. Amy, who was in the bow sheered off, but brought the side of the canoe skillfully against the rough planks.

"What are they doing to you, child?" Amy cried.

"Goin' to drown the witch! Goin' to drown the witch!" shrieked the rabble in the rear. "Spotted Snake! Spotted Snake!"

"It's little Henrietta!" screamed Jessie suddenly. "Oh, Amy!"

Amy, who was strong and quick, reached over the gunwale of the canoe and seized upon the crooked figure. She bore it inboard, knocking

off the old bonnet to reveal Henrietta's freckled
little face. The cloak and the hump under it
were likewise torn off and went sailing away on
the current.

"For pity's sake, Henrietta!" gasped Jessie.

"Yes'm," said the child composedly. "Did you
come to see me?"

"Not expecting to see you in this—this shape,"
hesitated Jessie.

Amy went off into a gale of laughter. She
could not speak for a minute. Jessie demanded:

"Who are those awful children, Henrietta?"

"Part Foleys, some McGuires, two Swansons,
the Costeklo twins, and Montmorency Shannon,"
was the literal reply.

"What were they trying to do to you?"

"Drown me," said Henrietta composedly. "But
they ain't ever done it yet. I always manage to get
away. I'm cute, I am. But once they most nearly
burned me, and Mrs. Foley stopped *that*. So now
they mostly try to drown the witch."

" 'The witch'?" murmured the amazed Jessie.

"Yep. That's me. Spotted Snake, the witch.
That's cause I'm so freckled. It's a great game."

"I should say it was," marveled Jessie, and
immediately Amy began to laugh again. "I don't
see how you can, Amy," Jessie complained. "I
think it is really terrible."

"I don't mind it," said Henrietta complacently.

"It keeps 'em busy and out from under their mothers' feet."

"But they shriek and yell so."

"That don't hurt 'em. And there's plenty of outdoors here to yell in. Where we moved from in town, folks complained of the Foleys because they made so much noise. But nobody ever complains here in Dogtown."

As Amy said, when she could keep from laughing, it was a great introduction to Henrietta's home. They went ashore, and Henrietta, who seemed to have a good deal of influence with the children, ordered two of the boys to watch the canoe and allow nobody to touch it. Then she proudly led the way to one of the largest and certainly the most decrepit looking of all the hovels in Dogtown.

Mrs. Foley, however, was a cheerful disappointment. She was, as Amy whispered, a "bulgy" person, but her calico wrapper was fairly clean; and although she sat down and took up her youngest to rock to sleep while she talked (being too busy a woman to waste any time visiting) she impressed the girls from Roselawn rather favorably.

"That child is the best young one in the world," Mrs. Foley confessed, referring to "Spotted Snake, the Witch." "Sometimes I rant at her like a good one. But she saves me a good bit, and if ever a child earned her keep, Hen earns hers."

Jessie asked about the missing cousin, Bertha..

"Bertha Blair. Yes. A good and capable girl. Was out at service when Hen's mother died and left her to me. Something's wrong with Bertha, or she surely would have come here to see Hen before this."

"Did Bertha Blair work for a woman named Poole?" Jessie asked.

"That I couldn't tell you, Miss. But you take Hen up to see your father, like you say you want to. The child's as sharp as a steel knife. Maybe she'll think of something that will put him on the trace of Bertha."

So they bore Spotted Snake away with them in the canoe, while the Dogtown gang shrieked farewells from the old landing. Henrietta had been dressed in a clean slip and the smartest hair ribbon she owned. But she had no shoes and stockings, those being considered unnecessary at Dogtown.

"I believe Nell could help us find something better for this child to wear," Amy observed, with more thoughtfulness than she usually displayed. "What do you think, Jess? Folks are always giving the Stanleys half-worn clothes for little Sally, more than Sally can ever make use of. And Hen is just about Sally Stanley's size."

"That might be arranged," agreed Jessie. "I guess you'd like to have a new dress, wouldn't you, Henrietta?"

"Oh, my yes! I know just what I would like," sighed Henrietta, clasping her clawlike hands. "You've seen them cape-suits that's come into fashion this year, ain't you? *That's* what I'd like."

"My dear!" gasped Amy explosively.

"I don't mind going barefooted," said Henrietta. "But if I could just have *one* dress in style! I expect you two girls wear lots of stylish things when you ain't wearing sweaters and over-all-pants like you did the other day. I never had anything stylish in my life."

Amy burst into delighted giggles, but Jessie said:

"The poor little thing! There is a lot in that. How should we like to wear nothing but second-hand clothes?"

" 'Hand me downs'," giggled Amy. "But mind you! A cape-coat suit! Can you beat it?"

"I saw pictures of 'em in a fashion book Mrs. McGuire sent for," went on Henrietta. "They are awful taking."

Little Henrietta proved to be an interesting specimen for the Norwood family that evening. Momsy took her wonted interest in so appealing a child. The serving people were curious and attentive. Mr. Norwood confessed that he was much amused by the young visitor.

A big dictionary placed in an armchair, raised little Henrietta to the proper height at the Norwood dinner table. Nothing seemed to trouble or astonish the visitor, either about the food or the service. And Jessie and Momsy wondered at the really good manners the child displayed.

Mrs. Foley had not wholly neglected her duty in Henrietta's case. And there seemed to be, too, a natural refinement possessed by the girl that aided her through what would have seemed a trying experience.

Best of all, Henrietta could give a good description of her missing cousin. Her name was Bertha Blair, and that was the name of the girl Mr. Norwood's clerk had interviewed before she had been whisked away by Martha Poole and Sadie Bothwell.

In addition, Mr. Norwood had brought home photographs of the two women, and both Jessie and Amy identified them as the women they had seen in Dogtown Lane, forcing the strange girl into the automobile.

"It is a pretty clear case," the lawyer admitted. "We know the date and the place where the missing witness was. But the thing is now to trace the movements of those women and their prisoner after they drove away from Dogtown Lane."

Nevertheless, he considered that every discovery, even a small one, was important. Detectives
would be started on the trail. Jessie and Amy
rode back to Dogtown in the Norwoods' car with
the excited Henrietta after dinner, leaving her
at the Foleys' with the promise that they would
see her soon again.

"And if those folks you know have any clothes
to give me," said Henrietta, longingly, "I hope
they'll be fashionable."

CHAPTER XVII

BROADCASTING

DARRY and Burd were planning another trip on the *Marigold,* and so had little time to give to the girl chums of Rose-lawn. Burd wickedly declared that Darry Drew was running away from home to get rid of Belle Ringold.

"Wherever he goes down town, she pops up like a jack-in-the-box and tries to pin him. Darry is so polite he doesn't know how to get away. But I know he wishes her mother would lock her in the nursery."

"It is her mother's fault that Belle is such a silly," scoffed Amy. "She lets Belle think she is quite grown up."

"She'll never be grown up," growled out Darry. "Never saw such a kid. If you acted like her, Sis, I'd put you back into rompers and feed you lollipops."

"You'd have a big chance doing anything like that to me, Master Darry," declared his sister, smartly. "Even Dad—bless his heart!—would not undertake to turn back the clock on me."

Before the two young fellows left Roselawn
again, they did the girls a favor that Amy and
Jessie highly appreciated. It was done involun-
tarily but was nevertheless esteemed. Mark
Stratford drifted up the Bonwit Boulevard in his
big and shiny car and halted it in front of the Norwood place to hail Darry and Burd.

"Here's the millionaire kid," called out Alling.
"Know him, girls? He's quite the fastest thing
that lingers about old Yale. Zoomed over the Ger-
man lines in the war, stoking an airplane, although
at that time he was only a kid. Mark Stratford.
His family are the Stratford Electric Company.
Oodles of money. But Mark is a patient soul."

" 'Patient'?" repeated Jessie, wonderingly, as
she and Amy accompanied the young fellows down
to the street.

"Sure," declared Burd. "Most fellows would
be impatient, burdened with so much of the filthy
lucre as Mark has. But not he. He is doing his
little best to spend his share."

However, and in spite of Burd's introduction,
Mark Stratford proved to be a very personable
young man and did not look at all the "sport."
Jessie considered that Burd was very probably
fooling them about Mark. The young folks were
talking like old friends in five minutes. In five
minutes more they had piled into the car for a
ride.

Mark's car "burned up the road" so fast that in half an hour they came to Stratfordtown where the huge plant of the Electric Company lay, and on the border of which was the large Stratford estate.

Jessie and Amy did not care anything about the beauties of the show place of the county. While riding over the girls had discussed one particular topic. And when Mark asked them where they wanted to go, or what they preferred to see, Jessie spoke out:

"Oh, Mr. Stratford! take us to the plant and let us go into the radio broadcasting room. Amy and I are just longing to see how it is done."

"Oh, *that!*" exclaimed Mark Stratford.

"We're crazy about radio, Mr. Stratford," agreed Amy.

"Some radio fiends, these two," said Darry. And he told his friend to what use the girls had already put Jessie's set for the benefit of the church bazaar.

"If you girls want to see how it's done, to be sure I'll introduce you to the man in charge. Wait till we drive around there." Stratford was as good as his word. It was a time in the afternoon when the Electric Company's matinee concert was being broadcasted. They went up in the passenger elevator in the main building of the plant to a sort of glassed-in roof garden. There were several rooms, or compartments, with glass partitions, sound-proof, and hung with curtains to cut off any echo. The young people could stare through the windows and see the performers in front of the broadcasting sets. The girls looked at each other and clung tightly to each other's hand.

"Oh, Amy!" sighed Jessie.

"If we could only get a chance to sing here!" whispered Amy in return.

It did not mean much to the boys. And Mark Stratford, of course, had been here time and time again. A gray-haired man with a bustling manner and wearing glasses came through the reception room and Mark stopped him.

"Oh, Mr. Blair!" the collegian said. "Here are some friends of mine who are regular radio bugs. Let me introduce you to Miss Jessie Norwood and Miss Amy Drew. Likewise," he added, as the gentleman smilingly shook hands with the girls, "allow me to present their comrades in crime, Darry Drew and Burdwell Alling. These fellows help me kill time over at Yale, to which the governor has sentenced me for four years."

"Mr. Blair?" repeated Jessie, looking sideways at her chum.

"Mr. Blair?" whispered Amy, who remembered the name as well as Jessie did.

"That is my name, young ladies," replied the superintendent, smiling.

"You don't know anything about a girl of our age named Blair, do you, Mr. Blair?" Jessie asked hesitatingly.

"I have no daughters," returned the superintendent, and the expression of his face changed so swiftly and so strangely that Jessie did not feel that she could make any further comment upon the thought that had stabbed her mind. After all, it seemed like sheer curiosity on her part to ask the man about his family.

"Just the same," she told Amy afterward, when they were in the automobile once more, "Blair is not such a common name, do you think?"

"But, of course, that Bertha Blair couldn't be anything to the superintendent of the broadcasting station. Oh, Jessie! What a wonderful program he had arranged for to-day. I am coming over to-night to listen in on that orchestral concert and hear Madame Elva sing. I would not miss it for anything."

"Suppose we could get a chance to help entertain!" Jessie sighed. "Not, of course, on the same program with such performers as these the Stratford people have. But——"

They happened to be traveling slowly and Mark overheard this. He twisted around in his seat to say:

"Why didn't you ask Blair about it? You have no idea how many amateurs offer their services. And some of them he uses."

"I'll say he does!" grumbled Burd. "Some of the singers and others I have listened in on have been punk."

"Well, I'll have you know that Jessie and I wouldn't sing if we could not sing well," Amy said, with spirit.

"Sure," agreed Burd, grinning. "Madame Elva wouldn't be a patch on you two girls singing the 'Morning Glories' Buns' or the 'Midnight Rolls'."

"Your taste in music is mighty poor, sure enough, Burd," commented Darry. "Jessie sings all right. She's got a voice like a——"

"Like a bird, I know," chuckled Alling. "That is just the way I sing—like a Burd."

"I've heard of a bird called a crow," put in Mark Stratford, smiling on the two girl chums. Jessie thought he had a really nice smile. "That is what your voice sounds like, Alling. You couldn't make the Glee Club in a hundred and forty years."

"Don't say a word!" cried Burd. "I'll be a long time past singing before the end of that term. Ah-ha! Here we are at Roselawn."

They got out at the Norwood place and the girls insisted upon Mark coming in to afternoon tea, which Amy and Jessie poured on the porch. The chums liked Mark Stratford and they did not believe that he was anywhere near as "sporty" as Burd had intimated. Naturally, a fellow who had driven a warplane and owned an airship now and often went up in it, would consider the driving of a motor-car rather tame. As for his college record, Jessie and Amy later discovered that Mark was a hard student and was at or near the head of his class in most of his studies.

"And he drives that wonderful car of his," said Amy, with approval, "like a jockey on the track."

The girl chums did not forget the concert they expected to enjoy that evening, but Darry and Burd left right after dinner for the moorings of the *Marigold* at City Island. They took Mark Stratford and some other college friends with them for a three days' trip on the yacht.

Jessie and Amy were eager to see the *Marigold;* but their parents had forbidden any mixed parties on the yacht until either Mr. and Mrs. Drew, or Mr. and Mrs. Norwood could accompany the young people. That would come later in the summer.

Amy ran over to the Norwood place before half past eight. The concert, Mr. Blair had told them, was to begin at nine. Jessie had learned a good deal about tuning in on the ether by this time; and there is no other part of radio knowledge more necessary if the operator would make full use of his set.

"The bedtime story is just concluded, Amy," Jessie said when her chum came in. "Sit down. I am going to get that talk on 'Hairpins and Haricots' by that extremely funny newspaper man— what is his name?"

"I don't know. What's in a name, anyhow?" answered her chum, lightly.

Amy adjusted the earphones while her friend manipulated the slides on the tuning coil. They did not catch the first of the talk, but they heard considerable of it. Then something happened— just what it was Amy had no idea. She tore off the eartabs and demanded:

"What *are* you doing, Jess? That doesn't sound like anything I ever heard before. Is it static interference?"

"It certainly is interference," admitted Jessie, trying to tune the set so as to get back upon the wave that had brought the funny talk about 'Hairpins and Haricots.'

But it did not work. Jessie could not get in touch with the lecture. Instead, out of the ether came one word, over and over again. And that word in a voice that Jessie was confident must come from a woman or a girl:

"Help! He-lp! He-e-lp!"

Over and over again it was repeated. Amy who had put on her head harness again, snatched at her chum's arm.

"Listen! Do you hear that?" she cried in an awed tone.

A Mystery of the Ether

CHAPTER XVIII

JESSIE knew that by carefully moving the slides on her tuning coil she could get into touch again with the talk to which she and Amy had been listening. But now the broadcasted cry for "Help!" seemed of so much importance that she wanted to hear more of this air mystery.

"He-lp!" The word came to their ears over and over again. Then: "I am a prisoner. They brought me here and locked me in. There is a red barn and silo and two fallen trees. He-lp! Come and find me!"

"For pity's sake, Jess Norwood!" shrilled Amy. "Do you hear that?"

"I'm trying to," her chum replied. "Hush!"

"It must be a hoax."

"Wait!"

They listened and heard it repeated, almost word for word. A red barn and a silo and two fallen trees. These points the strange voice insisted on with each repetition.

"I can't believe it!" declared Amy.

"It is a girl. I am sure it is a girl. Oh, Amy!"

gasped Jessie. "Suppose it should be the girl whom we saw carried off by those two awful women?"

"Bertha Blair?"

"Yes. Of course, I suppose that is awfully far-fetched——"

"Wait! Here it comes again," whispered Amy.

"Come and find me! Help! I am a prisoner! The red barn and the silo with the two fallen trees."

How many times this was repeated the girls did not know. Suddenly something cluttered up the airways—some sort of interference—and the mystery of the ether died away. No matter what Jessie did to the tuning coil she could not bring that strangely broadcasted message back to their ears.

"What do you know about that?" demanded Amy, breathlessly.

"Why—why," murmured her chum, "we don't know much of anything about it. Only, I am sure that was a girl calling. It was a youthful voice."

"And I feel that it is Bertha Blair!" exclaimed Amy. "Oh, Jessie, we must do something for her."

"How can we? How can we find her?"

"A red barn with a silo and two fallen trees. Think of it! Did you ever see a place like that when you have been riding about the country?"

"I—nev-er—did!" and Jessie shook her head despondently.

"But there must be such a place. It surely is not a hoax," said Amy, although at first she had thought it was a joke. "And there is another thing to mark, Jess."

"What is that?"

"The place where this girl is kept a prisoner has a broadcasting station. You can't talk into a radio set like this. There has to be electric power and a generator, and all that—such as Mark Stratford showed us there at Stratfordtown."

"Of course."

"Then don't you think, Jessie, the fact that it is a broadcasting plant where the girl is imprisoned must narrow the inquiry a good deal?"

"How clever you are, dear," declared Jessie. "But a red barn with a silo and two fallen trees! Why, Amy! we don't know in which direction to look. Whether to the north, south, east or west!"

"No-o. I suppose—— Oh, wait, Jess!" cried the excited Amy. "We don't really know where those women took that girl we saw carried off. They drove out the boulevard as far as we could see them. But, do you remember, we met that Mrs. Bothwell again in the big French car that very evening?"

"When we went to Parkville with Nell and

the Brandons!" Jessie said eagerly. "I remember she passed us. You pointed her out to me."

"And she turned out of the very road we took to go to Parkville," said Amy, with confidence. "I believe that red barn with the silo must be over beyond Parkville."

"It might be so," admitted her chum, thought fully. "I have never been through that section of the state. But Chapman knows every road, I guess."

"Doesn't your father know the roads, too?"

"But Daddy and Momsy have gone to Aunt Ann's in New York and will not be back to-night," Jessie explained.

"Anyhow we couldn't go hunting around in the dark after this broadcasting station, wherever it is," Amy observed.

"Of course not," her chum agreed, taking the harness off her head. "Come down to the telephone and I'll see if Chapman is in the garage."

They ran downstairs, forgetting all about the radio concert they were to have heard, and Jessie called up the garage to which a private wire was strung.

The chauffeur, who had served the Norwoods ever since they had had a car, answered Jessie's request quickly, and appeared at the side door. Amy was just as eager as Jessie to cross-question the man about a red barn with a silo. He had to ask the girls to stop and begin all over again, and——

"If you please, Miss Jessie," he added, widely a-grin, "either let Miss Amy tell me or you tell me. I can't seem to get it right when you both talk."

"Oh, I am dumb!" announced Amy. "Go ahead, Jess; you tell him."

So Jessie tried to put the case as plainly as possible; but from the look on Chapman's face she knew that the chauffeur thought that this was rather a fantastic matter.

"Why, Chapman!" she cried, "you do not know much about this radio business, do you?"

"Only what I have seen of it here, Miss Jessie. I heard the music over your wires. But I did not suppose that anybody could talk into the thing and other folks could hear like——"

"Oh! You don't understand," Jessie interrupted. "No ordinary radio set broadcasts. It merely receives."

As clearly as she could she explained what sort of plant there must be from which the strange girl had sent out her cry for help.

"Of course, you understand, the girl must have got a chance on the sly to speak into the broadcasting horn. Now, all the big broadcasting stations are registered with the Government. And if secret ones are established the Government agents soon find them out.

"It might be, if the people who imprisoned this girl are the ones we think, they may have a plant for the sending out of information that is illegal. For instance, it might have some connection with race track gambling. One of the women is interested in racing and the other in automobile contests. If the broadcasting plant is near a race course or an autodrome——"

"Now you give me an idea, Miss Jessie!" exclaimed Chapman suddenly. "I remember a stock farm over behind Parkville where the barns are painted red. And there is a silo or two. Besides, it is near the Harrimay Race Course. I could drive over there in the morning, if you want to go. Mr. Norwood won't mind, I am sure."

"Would you go, Amy?" Jessie asked, hesitatingly.

"Sure! It's a chance. And I am awfully anxious now to find out what that mysterious voice means."

A Puzzling Circumstance
Something Doing at the Stanley's

CHAPTER XIX

JESSIE'S parents being away, Amy ran home and announced her desire to keep her chum company and was back again before ten o'clock. There was not much to be heard over the airways after that hour. They had missed Madame Elva and the orchestra music broadcasted from Stratfordtown.

"Nothing to do but to go to bed," Amy declared. "The sooner we are asleep the sooner we can get up and go looking for the mysterious broadcasting station. Do you believe that cry for help was from little Hen's cousin?"

"I have a feeling that it is," Jessie admitted.

"Maybe we ought to take Spotted Snake, the Witch, with us," chuckled her chum. "What do you say?"

"I think not, honey. We might only raise hopes in the child's mind that will not be fulfilled. I think she loves her cousin Bertha very much; and of course we do not know that this is that girl whose cry for help we heard."

"We don't really know anything about it. Maybe it is all a joke or a mistake."

149

"Do you think that girl sounded as though she were joking?" was Jessie's scornful reply. "Anyway, we will look into it alone first. If Chapman can find the stock farm with the red barn——"

"And there are two fallen trees and a silo near it," put in Amy, smiling. "Goodness me, Jess! I am afraid the boys would say we had another crazy notion."

"I like that!" cried Jessie Norwood. "What is there crazy about trying to help somebody who certainly must be in trouble? Besides," she added very sensibly, "Daddy Norwood will be very thankful to us if we should manage to find that Bertha Blair. He needs her to witness for his clients, and Momsy says the hearing before the Surrogate cannot be postponed again. The matter must soon be decided, and without Bertha Blair's testimony Daddy's clients may lose hundreds of thousands of dollars."

"We'll be off to the rescue of the prisoner in the morning, then," said Amy, cuddling down into one of her chum's twin beds. "Good-night! Sweet dreams! And if you have a nightmare don't expect me to get up and tie it to the bedpost."

The next morning Chapman brought around the car as early as half past eight, when the girls were just finishing breakfast.

"Don't eat any more, Amy," begged Jessie. "Do

get up for once from the table feeling that you could eat more. The doctors say that is the proper way."

"Pooh! What do the doctors know about eating?" scoffed Amy. "Their job is to tend to you when you can't eat. Why? honey! I feel lots better morally with a full stomach than when I am hungry."

They climbed into the car and Chapman drove out the boulevard and turned into the Parkville road. It was a lovely morning, not too hot and with only a wind made by their passage, so that the dust only drifted behind the car. They passed the home of Mr. and Mrs. Brandon's daughter and saw the aerials strung between the house and the flagpole on the garage.

"Keep your eyes open for aerials anywhere, Amy," said Jessie. "Of course wherever that broadcasting station is, the aerials must be observable."

"They'll be longer and more important than the antenna for the usual receiving set, won't they?" eagerly asked Amy.

"Of course." Then Jessie leaned forward to speak to Chapman, for they were in the open car. "When you approach the stock farm you spoke of, please drive slowly. We want to look over all the surroundings."

"Very well, Miss Jessie," the chauffeur said.

Passing through Parkville, they struck a road called a turnpike, although there were no ticket-houses, as there are at the ferries. It was an old highway sweeping between great farms, and the country was rolling, partly wooded, and not so far off the railroad line that the latter did not touch the race-track Chapman had spoken of.

The car skirted the high fence of the Harrimay enclosure and then they ran past a long string of barns in which the racing horses were housed and trained for a part of the year. There was no meet here at this time, and consequently few horses were in evidence.

"I like to see horses race," remarked Amy. "And they are such lovely, intelligent looking creatures. But so many people who have anything to do with horses and racing are such hard-faced people and so—so impossible! Think of the looks of that Martha Poole. She's the limit, Jessie."

"Neither she nor Mrs. Bothwell is nice, I admit. But don't blame it on the poor horses," Jessie observed, smiling. "I am sure it is not their fault. Mrs. Poole would be objectionable if she was interested in cows—or—or Pekingese pups."

Chapman turned up a hilly road and they came out on a ridge overlooking the fenced-in track. The chauffeur shifted his position so as to glance behind him at the girls, the car running slowly.

"Now look out, Miss Jessie," he advised. "We are coming to the old Gandy stock farm. That's the roof of the house just ahead. Yonder is the tower they built to house the electric lighting plant like what your father used to have. See it?"

"Yes, yes!" exclaimed Jessie. "But—but I don't see any aerials. No, I don't! And the red barn——"

"There it is!" cried Amy, grabbing at her chum's arm. "With the silo at the end."

The car turned a corner in the road and the entrance gate to the estate came into view. Up the well kept lane, beyond the rambling house of weathered shingles, stood a long, low barn and a silo, both of a dull red color. And on either side of the entrance gate were two broken willow trees, their tall tops partly removed, but most of the trunks still lying upon the ground where they had fallen.

"Ha!" ejaculated the chauffeur. "Those trees broke down since I was past here last."

"Do drive slower, Chapman," Jessie cried.

But she drew Amy down when the girl stood up to stare at the barn and the tower.

"There may be somebody on watch," Jessie hissed. "They will suspect us. And if it is either of those women, they will recognize you."

"Cat's foot!" ejaculated Amy. "I don't see any signs of occupancy about the house. Nor is there anybody working around the place. It looks abandoned."

"We don't know. If the poor girl is shut up here——"

"Where?" snapped Amy.

"Perhaps in the house."

"Perhaps in the barn," scoffed her chum. "Anyway, every window of that tower, both the lower and the upper stories, is shuttered on the outside."

"Maybe that is where Bertha is confined—if it is Bertha."

"But, honey! Where is the radio? There is nothing but a telephone wire in sight. There is no wireless plant here."

"Dear me, Amy! don't you suppose we have come to the right place?"

The car was now getting away from the Gandy premises. Jessie had to confess that there was no suspicious looking wiring anywhere about the house or outbuildings.

"It does not seem as though that could be the place after all. What do you think, Chapman?" she added, leaning forward again. "Don't you think that place looked deserted?"

"It often does between racing seasons, Miss Jessie," the man said. "Whoever owns it now does not occupy it all the year."

Suddenly Jessie sat up very straight and her

face flamed again with excitement.   She cried aloud:

"Chapman!   Isn't there a village near?   And a real estate office?"

"Harrimay is right over the hills, Miss Jessie," said the chauffeur.

"Drive there at once, please," said the girl. "And stop at the office of the first real estate agent whose sign you see."

"For goodness sake, Jess!" drawled Amy, her eyes twinkling, "you don't mean to buy the Gandy farm, do you?"

CHAPTER XX

C HAPMAN drove the automobile down into Harrimay only ten minutes later. It
was a pretty but rather somnolent place,
just a string of white-painted, green-blinded houses
and two or three stores along both sides of an
oiled highway. It was a long ten-minute jitney
ride from the railway station.

"Perkins, Real Estate" faced the travelers
from a signboard as they drove into the village.
Chapman stopped before the office door, and the
eager Jessie hopped out.

"I'm coming, too! I'm coming, too!" squealed
Amy, running across the walk after her.

"Do be quiet," begged her chum. "And for
once let me do the talking."

"Oui, oui, Mademoiselle! As I haven't the
least idea what the topic of the conversation will
be, I can easily promise that," whispered Amy.

A high-collared man with eyeglasses and an
ingratiating smile arose from behind a flat-topped
desk facing the door and rubbed his hands as he
addressed the two girls.

"What can I do for you, young ladies?"

"Why, why—— Oh, I want to ask you—"
Jessie stammered. "Do you know who owns the
farm over there by the track? The Gandy
place?"

"The old Gandy stock farm, Miss?" asked the
real estate man with a distinct lowering of tone.
"It is not in the market. The Gandy place never
has been in the market."

"I just wish to know who owns it," repeated
Jessie, while Amy stared.

"The Gandys still own it. At least old man
Gandy's daughter is in possession I believe. Horse
people, all of them. This woman——"

"Please tell me her name?"

"Poole, Martha Poole, is her name."

"Oh!" cried Amy, seeing now what Jessie
wanted.

But Jessie shook her head at her chum warn-
ingly, and asked the man:

"Do you know if Mrs. Poole is at the place
now?"

"Couldn't say. She comes and goes. She is
always there when the racing is going on. It is
supposed that some things that go on there at the
Gandy place are not entirely regular," said the
real estate man stiffly. "If you are a friend of
Mrs. Poole——"

"I am Jessie Norwood. My father, Mr. Robert Norwood, is a lawyer, and we live in the Rose-lawn section of New Melford."

"Oh, ah, indeed!" murmured the real estate man. "Then I guess it is safe to tell you that the people around here do not approve of Mrs. Poole and what goes on at the Gandy place during the racing season. It is whispered that people there are interested in pool rooms in the city. You know, where betting on the races is conducted."

"I do not know anything about that," replied Jessie, in some excitement. "But I thank you for telling me about Martha Poole."

She seized Amy by the arm and hurried back to the automobile.

"What do you think of that?" gasped Amy, quite as much amazed as was her chum.

"I do wish Daddy was coming home to-day. But he isn't. Not until dinner time, anyway. I do believe, Amy Drew, that poor Bertha is hidden away somewhere at that farm."

"But—but——how could she get at any sending station to tell her troubles to—to the air?" and Amy suddenly giggled.

"Don't laugh. It is a very serious matter, I feel sure. If the poor girl actually isn't being abused, those women are hiding her away so that they can cheat Daddy's clients out of a lot of money."

"Again I ask," repeated Amy, more earnestly,

"*how* could that girl, whoever she is, get to a sending station? We did not see the first sign of an
aerial anywhere near that house and barn, or
above the tower, either."

"I don't know what it means. It is a mystery,"
confessed Jessie. "But I just *feel* that what we
heard over the radio had to do with that missing
girl—that it was Bertha Blair calling for help,
and that in some way she is connected with that
red barn and the silo and the two fallen trees. We
traced the place from her description."

"So we did!"

"And unless it is all a big hoax, somewhere
near that place Bertha is held a prisoner. If that
Martha Poole is in with some crooked people
who break the state gambling law by radio, sending news of the races to city gambling rooms,
she would commit other things against the law."

"Oh!" cried Amy. "Both she and that Mrs.
Bothwell look like hard characters. But there
were no aerials in sight!"

Jessie thought for a moment. Then she flashed
at her chum:

"Well, that might be, too. Some people string
their aerials indoors. I don't know if that can
be done at a sending station. But it may be.
They are inventing new things about radio all
the time. You know that, dear."

"I know it," agreed Amy.

"And if that broadcasting station up there at the Gandy farm is used for the sending of private racing information, in all probability the people who set it up would want to keep it secret."

"I see! So they would."

"It is not registered, you can make up your mind. And as it is only used much when the racing season is on at the Harrimay track, the Government has probably given it little attention."

"Could they find it, do you think, Jessie?" asked her chum.

"I have read that the Government has wonderful means of locating any 'squeak-box', as they call it, that is not registered and which litters up the airways with either unimportant or absolutely evil communications. These methods of tracing unregistered sending stations were discovered during the war and were proved thoroughly before the Government allowed any small stations to be established since."

"Do you suppose the police knew that that woman was sending racing news to gambling rooms from up there at her farm?"

"We don't know that she is. Mr. Perkins was only repeating gossip. And we did not see aerials up there."

"But you say that maybe they could have rigging for the station without any aerials in the open?"

"It might be. I am all confused. There certainly is a mystery about it, and Daddy Norwood ought to know at once. Oh, Chapman! That was thunder. We must hurry home."

"Yes, Miss Jessie," said the chauffeur, looking up at the clouds that had been gathering. "I think I can get you home before it rains."

He increased the speed of the car. They had circled around by another way than the Parkville road, and they came through the edge of New Melford. When the automobile shot into Bonwit Boulevard and headed toward Roselawn the first flash of lightning made the girls jump.

Chapman stepped on the accelerator and the car shot up the oiled way. The thunder seemed to explode right overhead. Before the first peal rolled away there was another sharp flash. Although the rain still held off, the tempest was near.

"Oh!" gasped Jessie, covering her eyes.

"There's the church," said Amy. "We'll soon be home now."

Even as she spoke another crackling stroke burst overhead. The green glare of it almost blinded them. The thunder shook the air. Jessie screamed.

"See! See! Look at the parsonage!" she cried in Amy's ear.

"Why, the boys must have already strung their

wires and got a radio set established," said Amy.

"Look at the window—that attic window!" Jessie exclaimed. "Don't you see what I see, Amy Drew?"

"It's smoke!" said the other girl, amazed.

"The house is afire! In the attic! That lightning must have struck there. It must have been led in by the wires, just as Momsy feared."

"Then the boys never closed their switch!" cried Amy. "Oh! I wonder if Doctor Stanley or Nell knows that the house is on fire?"

CHAPTER XXI

A GREAT TO-DO

"CHAPMAN! Stop!" shouted Jessie. "We must tell them!"

The chauffeur wheeled the car in toward the curb and stopped as quickly as he could. But it was some distance past the church and the parsonage.

The girls jumped out and ran back. They saw Dr. Stanley come out on the porch from his study. He was in his house gown and wore a little black cap to cover his bald spot. It was a little on one side and gave the good clergyman a decidedly rakish appearance.

"Come in here, children! Hurry! It is going to rain," he called in his full and mellow voice.

"Oh, Doctor! Doctor!" Jessie gasped. "The fire! The fire!"

"Why, you are not wet. Here come the first drops. You don't need a fire."

"Nor you don't need one, Doctor," and Amy began to laugh. "But you've got one just the same."

"In the kitchen stove. Is it a joke or a conun-

drum?" asked the smiling minister, as the two
chums came up under the porch roof just as the
first big drops came thudding down.

"Upstairs! The radio!" declared the earnest
Jessie. "Don't you know it's afire?"

"The radio afire?"

"The lightning struck it. Didn't you feel and
hear it? The boys must have left the switch to
the receiver open, and the lightning came right
in——"

"Come on!" broke in Amy, who knew the way
about the parsonage as well as she did about her
own house. "We saw the smoke pouring out of
the window," and she darted in and started up
the front stairway.

"Why, why!" gasped the good doctor. "I can
hardly believe Nell would be so careless."

"Oh, it isn't Nell," Jessie said, following her
chum. "It is the boys."

"But she always knows what the boys are up
to, and Sally, too," declared the minister, confident of his capable daughter's oversight of the
family.

The girls raced up the two flights. They
smelled the smoke strongly as they mounted the
second stairway to the garret. Then they heard
voices.

"They've got it right in the old lumber room,
Jess!" panted Amy.

"But why don't they give the alarm?"

"Trying to put it out themselves. We ought to have brought buckets!"

"There is no water on this floor!"

Amy banged open the door of the big room in which they knew, by the arrangement of the out- side wires, Bob and Fred must have set up the radio set. Amy plunged in, with Jessie right be- hind her. The room was unpleasantly filled with smoke.

"Why don't you put it out?" shrieked Amy, and then began to cough.

"Hullo!" Bob Stanley exclaimed out of the smother. "We want to put it in, not out. Hullo, Jess. You here, too?"

"The fire! The smoke!" gasped Jessie.

"Shucks," said Fred, who was down on his knees poking at something. "We can't have the windows open, for the rain is beating this way. We've got to solder this thing. Did you have trouble with yours, Jess?"

"Sweetness and daylight!" groaned a voice be- hind them.

Dr. Stanley stood in the doorway. He was a heavy man, and mounting the stairs at such a pace tried his temper as well as his wind.

"Is *this* what started you girls off at such a tearing pace? Why, the boys borrowed that sol- dering outfit from the plumber. It's all right."

"I am so sorry we annoyed you," said Jessie, contritely.

But Amy had begun to laugh and could say nothing. Only waved her hands weakly and looked at the clergyman, whose cap was much more over his ear than before.

"Right in the middle of Sunday's sermon, young ladies," said the minister, with apparent sternness. "If that sermon is a failure, Amy and Jessie, I shall call on one of you girls—perhaps both of you—to step up into the pulpit and take my place. Remember that, now!" and he marched away in apparent dudgeon; but they heard him singing "Onward Christian Soldiers" before he got to the bottom of the upper flight of stairs.

"But it certainly was a great to-do," murmured Jessie, as she tried to see what the boys were doing.

She was able to advise them after a minute. But Amy insisted upon opening one of the windows and so getting more of the smoke out of the long room.

"You boys don't even know how to make a fire in a fire-pot without creating a disturbance," she said.

Nell came up from the kitchen where she had been consulting the cook about the meals, and Sally came tagging after her, of course, with a cookie in one hand and a rag doll in the other.

"This Sally is nothing but a yawning cavity walking on hollow stilts," declared Nell, who "fussed" good-naturedly, just as her father did. "She is constantly begging from the cook between meals, and her eyes are the biggest things about her when she comes to the table."

"Ain't," said Sally, shaking her curls in denial.

"Ain't what?" asked Jessie.

"Ain't—ain't *if you please*," declared the little girl, revealing the fact that her sister had tried to train her in politeness.

When the girls stopped laughing—and Sally had finished the cookie—Nell added:

"Aunt Freda came last night to dinner and we had strawberry fool. Cook makes a delicious one. And Sally could eat her weight of that delicacy. When I came to serve the dessert Sally was watching me with her eagle eye and her mouth watering. I spooned out an ordinary dishful, and Sally whispered:

" 'Oh, sister! is *that* all I get?'

"So I told her it was for Aunt Freda, and she gasped:

" 'What! All *that?*' "

The boys got the thing they wanted soldered completed about this time, and Bob ran down the back way with the fire-pot. The rain began to lift. As Nell cheerfully said, a patch of blue sky soon appeared in the west big enough to make a Scotchman a kilt, so they could be sure that it would clear.

Jessie and Amy walked home after seeing the Stanley boys' radio set completed. Their minds then naturally reverted to the adventures of the morning and what they had heard so mysteriously out of the ether the evening before. Jessie had warned her chum to say nothing to anybody about the mysterious prisoner and the stock farm over by Harrimay or of their suspicions until she had talked again with Mr. Norwood.

Momsy came home that afternoon from Aunt Ann's, but Mr. Norwood did not appear. The Court was sitting, and he had several cases which needed his entire attention. He often remained away from home several days in succession at such times.

"And one of the most important cases is that one he told us about," Momsy explained. "He is greatly worried about that. If he cannot find that girl who lived with Mrs. Poole——"

"Oh, Momsy!" exclaimed Jessie, "let us find Daddy and tell him about what Amy and I heard over the radio. I believe we learned something about Bertha Blair, only we could not find her this morning."

She proceeded to explain the adventure which included the automobile trip to Harrimay and

the Gandy farm. Momsy became excited. It did
not really seem to her to be so; but she agreed
that Daddy Norwood ought to hear about it.

When they tried to get him on the long distance
telephone, however, the Court had closed for the
day and so had the Norwood law office. He was
not at his club, and Momsy did not know at which
hotel he was to spend the night. There
really seemed to be nothing more Jessie could do
about the lost witness. And yet she feared that
this delay in getting her father's attention would
be irreparable.

CHAPTER XXII

SILK!

BELLE RINGOLD and Sally Moon came up to the Norwood place the next forenoon and found Jessie and Amy in a porch hammock, their heads together, writing a letter to Jessie's father. Jessie had tried to get Robert Norwood at his office right after breakfast, but a clerk had informed her that Mr. Norwood was not expected there until later. He would go direct to court from his hotel.

"And they have no more idea where he went to sleep than Momsy had," Jessie had explained to her chum when Amy appeared, eager and curious. "He is so busy with his court work that he does not want to be disturbed, I know. But it seems to me that what we heard over the radio ought to be told to him."

It was Amy who had suggested the writing of the letter and having it taken into town by Chapman, the chauffeur. The coming of Belle and Sally disturbed the chums in the middle of the letter.

"Glad we found you here, Amy," said Belle. "You never are at home, are you?"

"Only to sleep," confessed Amy Drew. "What seems to be the trouble, ladies? Am I not to be allowed to go calling?"

"Oh, we know you are always gadding over here," said Sally, laughing. "You are Jessie's shadow."

"Ha, ha! and likewise ho, ho!" rejoined Amy. "In this case then, the shadow is greater than the substance. I weigh fifteen pounds more than Jess. We'll have to see about that."

"And I suppose your brother, Darrington, is over here, too?" asked Belle, her sharp eyes glancing all about the big veranda.

"Wrong again," rejoined Amy, cheerfully. "But if you have any message for Darry you can trust me to deliver it to him."

"Where is he?"

"Just about off Barnegat, if his plans matured," said Amy composedly.

"Oh!" cried Belle. "Did he go out on that yacht? And without taking any of us girls?" and she began to pout.

"No mixed parties until the family can go along," Amy said promptly. "Jess and I, even, haven't been aboard the *Marigold*."

"Oh, you children!" scoffed Belle. "I shouldn't think that Darry and Burd Alling and that Mark

Stratford would want little girls tagging them.
Why, they are in college."

Belle really was a year older than the chums;
but she acted, and seemed to feel, as though she
were grown up. Amy stared at her with wide
eyes.

"Well, I like your nerve!" said she. "Darry's
my brother. And I've known Burd Alling since
he and Darry went to primary school. And so
has Jess. I guess they are not likely to take
strangers off on that yacht with them before they
take Jess and me."

Belle tossed her head and laughed just as
though she considered Amy's heated reply quite
childish.

"Oh, dear me," she proclaimed. "To hear
you, one would think you were still playmates, all
making mud pies together. I don't know that you
and Jess, Amy Drew, ever will be grown up."

"Hope not, if we have to grow into anything
that looks and acts like you," grumbled Amy.

But Jessie tried to pour oil on the troubled
waters. "Just what did you come for, Belle?" she
asked. After all, she must play hostess. "Is it
anything I can do for you?"

Some of us older girls are going to have a box
party down at the Carter Landing on Lake
Monenset the first moonlight night. Sally and I
are on the committee of arrangements. We want

to talk it over with Darrington and Burd and get them to invite Mark Stratford."

"Humph!" You'll have to use long distance or radio," chuckled Amy.

"Now, don't interfere, Amy!" said Belle sharply.

"Wait," Jessie said, in her quiet way. "Don't let us argue over nothing. The boys really are off on their boat. We do not know just when they are coming back. Why don't you write Darry a note and leave it at the house?"

"Humph! I wonder if he'd get it?" snapped Belle, with her face screwed up as though she had bitten into something awfully sour.

"Well! I like her impudence," muttered Amy, as Belle and Sally disappeared. "I don't see how her mother ever let her grow up."

"It is not as bad as all that," her chum said gravely. "But it is awfully silly for Belle and those girls who go with her to be thinking of the boys all the time, and trying to get the older boys to show an interest in them. That is perfectly ridiculous."

"You're right," said Amy, bluntly. "And Darry and Burd think that Belle is foolish."

"Now, let's finish this letter to Daddy," Jessie said, hastily. "And then, oh, Amy Drew, I have an idea!"

"Another idea?" cried her friend.

"I don't know whether there is anything in it or not. But listen. Don't you think we might get Henrietta, take her over to the Gandy place, and look around again for Bertha?"

"We-ell, I admit that kid has got sharp eyes. But how could she see into those buildings that are all shut up any better than we could when we were over there?"

"You don't just get my idea, honey. If the girl who radioed her message, and which we heard, is Henrietta's cousin, she will know Henrietta's voice. And if Henrietta calls her from outside, maybe she can shout and we will hear her."

"That is an idea!" exclaimed Amy. "It might work, at that." Then she laughed. "Anyway, we can give Hen a ride. Hen certainly likes riding in an automobile."

"And Nell has got an almost new dress and other things for her. Let us go down to the parsonage and get them. And while Chapman goes to town with this letter we'll paddle around to Dogtown and get Henrietta."

"Fine!" cried Amy, and ran home for her hat.

A little later, when she had returned from the parsonage with the bundle and the chums were embarked upon the lake, Jessie said:

"I hope the poor little thing will like this dress that Nell was so kind as to find for her. But, to tell the truth, Amy, it seems a little old for Henrietta."

"Is it a cape-coat suit?" giggled her friend.

"It is a little taffeta silk, and Nell said it was cut in a style so disgracefully freakish that she would not let Sally wear it. It was bought at one of those ultra-shops on Fifth Avenue where they have styles for children that ape the frocks their big sisters wear."

"Let's see it," urged Amy, with curiosity.

"Wait till you see it on Henrietta. There are undies, too, and stockings and a pair of shoes that I hope will fit her. But consider! Taffeta silk for a child like Henrietta."

There could be no doubt that the girls from Roselawn were welcome when they landed at Dogtown and came to the Foley house. The greater number of the village children seemed to have swarmed elsewhere; but little Henrietta was sitting on the steps of the house holding the next-to-the-youngest Foley in her arms.

"Hush!" she hissed, holding up an admonishing finger. "He's 'most gone. When he goes I'll lay him in that soap-box and cover him with the mosquito netting. Then I can tend to you."

"The little, old-fashioned thing," murmured Amy. "It isn't right, Jess."

Jessie understood and nodded. She was glad that Amy showed a certain amount of sympathy for Henrietta and appreciation of her. In a few moments the child was utterly relaxed and Henrietta got up and staggered over to the soap-box on wheels and laid the sleeper down upon a pillow.

"He ought to sleep an hour," said little Henrietta, covering Billy Foley carefully so that the flies could not bite his fat, red legs. "I ain't got nothing to do now but to sweep out the house, wash the dishes in the sink, clean the clinkers out of the stove, hang out a line for clothes, and make the beds before Mrs. Foley and the baby get back. I can talk to you girls while I'm doing them things."

"Landy's sake!" gasped Amy, horrified

But Jessie determined to take matters in her own hands for the time being, Mrs. Foley not being present. She immediately unrolled the bundle of things she had brought, and Henrietta halted on the step of the house, poised as though for flight, her pale eyes gradually growing rounder and rounder.

"Them ain't for *me?*"

"If they fit you, or can be made to fit you, honey," said Jessie.

"Oh, the poor child!" exclaimed Amy softly, taking care that Henrietta should not hear her.

"Silk!" murmured Henrietta, and sat down on the step again, put her arms out widely and squeezed the silk dress up to her flat little body as though the garment was another baby.

"Silk!" repeated the poor little thing. "Miss Jessie! How good you are to me! I never did have a thing made of silk before, 'cepting a hair-ribbon. And I never had any too many of them."

CHAPTER XXIII

DARRY'S BIG IDEA

WHEN Mrs. Foley and the baby arrived home there stood upon the platform at the back door of the house a most amazing figure. She knew every child in Dogtown, and none of them had ever made such an appearance. She almost dropped the baby through amazement.

"For love of John Thomas McGuire!" burst forth the "bulgy" woman, finally finding her voice. "What's happened to that child? Is it an angel she's turned into? Or is she an heiress, I dunno? Hen Haney! what's the meaning of this parade? And have you washed the dishes like I told you?"

"You must forgive her, Mrs. Foley," Jessie said, coming down to meet the woman and taking the baby from her. "Go and see and speak to the child," she whispered. "She is so delighted that she has not been able to talk for ten minutes."

"Then," said Mrs. Foley solemnly, "the wor-r-rld has come to an end. When Hen Haney can't talk——"

But she mounted heavily to the platform. Little

Henrietta stood there like a wax figure. She dared not move for fear something would happen to her finery.

Every individual freckle on her thin, sharp face seemed to shine as though there was some radiance behind it. Absurd as that taffeta dress was for a child of her age, it seemed to her an armor against all disaster. Nothing bad (she had already acclaimed it to Amy and Jessie) could happen to her with that frock on. And those silk stockings! And the patent-toed shoes! And a hat that almost hid the child's features from view!

"Well, well, well!" muttered the amazed Mrs. Foley. "If anybody had ever told me that you'd have been dressed up like—like a millionaire's kid! When I took you away from your poor dead mother and brought you out here, Hen Haney, to be a playfellow of me little Charlie, and Billy, and—and—Well, anyway, to be a playmate to them. Ha! You never cleaned out the stove-grate, did you?"

She had looked into the kitchen and saw the dishes in the sink and the gaping stove hearth, and shook her head. Jessie thought it time to intercede for the little girl.

"You must forgive her, Mrs. Foley, and blame me. I made her dress up in the things we brought. I was sure you would want to see her in her Sunday clothes."

A deep sigh welled up from Henrietta's chest. "Am I going to sure-enough keep 'em to wear Sundays?" she asked.

"If Mrs. Foley will let you," said the politic Jessie. "You can keep them very carefully. It is really wonderful how well they fit."

"Sure," sighed Mrs. Foley, "she's better dressed than me own children."

"But you told us your children were all boys," Amy put in quickly.

"Aw, but a time like this I wish't I had a daughter," declared the woman, gazing at Henrietta almost tenderly. "What a sweet little colleen she might be if she had some flesh on her bones and something besides freckles to color her face. Yes, yes!"

"I am awfully glad, Mrs. Foley," said Jessie quickly, "to see how much you approve of what we have tried to do for Henrietta. So I am bold enough to ask you to let us take her up to my house for over night. Momsy wants to see her in these new clothes, and——"

"Well, if Mrs. Momsy—Or is it Mr. Momsy, I dunno?"

"Why, Momsy is my mother!"

"The like o' that now! And she lets you call her out o' name? Well, there is no understanding you rich folks. Ha! So you want to take little Hen away from me?"

"Only for over night.   It would be a little vacation for her, you know."

Mrs. Foley looked back into the kitchen and shook her head.   "By the looks o' things," she said, "she's been having a vacation right here. Well, she'll be no good for a while anyway, I can see that.   Why, she can't much more than speak with them glad rags on her."

"Come on," said Henrietta, and walked down the steps, heading toward the lake.

Amy burst into laughter again, and even Mrs. Foley began to grin.

"She's as ready to go as though you two young ladies was her fairy god-mothers.   Sure, and maybe 'tis me own fault.   I've been telling her for years about the Good Little People that me grandmother knew in Ireland—or said she knew, God rest her soul! — and she has always been looking for banshees and ha'nts and fairies to appear and whisk her away.   She is a princess in disguise that's been char-r-rmed by a wicked witch. All them stories and beliefs has kept her contented.   She's a good little thing," Mrs. Foley ended, wiping her eyes.   "Go along with her and tell your Mrs. Momsy to be good to her."

So they got away from Dogtown with flying colors.   Henrietta sat, a little silk-clad figure, in the bottom of the canoe and shivered whenever she thought a drop of water might come inboard.

"She ought to have worn her old clothes in the canoe," Amy suggested, but with dancing eyes.

"O-o-oh!" gasped Henrietta, pleadingly.

"It is going to take dentist's forceps to ever get the child out of that dress," chuckled Jessie. "I can see that."

They got back to Roselawn in good season for dinner. Chapman had returned from town, but had not brought Mr. Norwood home. Jessie's father, it seemed, had left the courtroom early in the afternoon and had gone out of town on some matter connected with the Ellison case. That case, as Jessie and her mother feared, was already in the court. A jury had been decided upon, as the defendants, Mrs. Poole and Mrs. Bothwell, had been advised by McCracken, their lawyer, to demand a jury trial.

The plaintiffs would have to get in their witnesses the next day. If Bertha Blair was ever to aid the side of right and truth in this matter, she must be found and brought to court.

"And we don't know how to find her. If she is hidden away over there at that Gandy farm, how shall we ever find it out for sure?" wailed Jessie. "I hoped Daddy would get my letter and come and take charge of the search himself."

"Your idea of taking Henrietta over there and letting her call Bertha is a good one," declared Amy stubbornly. "Aren't you going to do it?"

"Yes. We'll drive over early. But it is only a chance."

They could not interest Henrietta in her Cousin Bertha that evening, save that she said she hoped Bertha would come and see her before she had to take off the silk dress and the other articles of her gay apparel.

She scarcely had appetite for dinner, although Momsy and Jessie tried their very best to interest Henrietta in several dishes that were supposed to appeal to a child's palate. Henrietta was polite and thanked them, but was not enthusiastic.

She found a tall mirror in the drawing room and every time they missed her, Jessie tiptoed into that long apartment to see Henrietta posing before the glass. The child certainly did enjoy her finery.

The suggestion of bedtime only annoyed Henrietta. But finally Jessie took her upstairs and showed her the twin beds in her own room, one of which the visitor was to occupy, and so gradually Henrietta came to the idea that some time she would have to remove the new clothes.

They listened in on the radio that evening until late, using the amplifier and horn that Mr. Norwood had bought. Henrietta could not understand how the voices could come into the room over the outside wires.

"I'll tell Charlie Foley and Montmorency

Shannon about this," she confided to Jessie and
Amy. "I guess you don't know them. But they
are smart. They can rig one of these wireless
things with wires, I bet. And then the whole of
Dogtown will listen in."

"Or, say! Maybe they won't let poor folks
like those in Dogtown have radios? Will they?"

"This is for the rich and poor alike," Jessie
assured her.

"Provided," added Amy, "that the poor are
not too poor."

They finally got Henrietta to bed. She went to
sleep with the silk dress hanging over a chair
within reach. After Amy had gone home Jessie
retired with much more worriment upon her
mind than little Henrietta had upon hers.

Everybody was astir early about the Norwood
and Drew places in Roselawn that next morning.
At the former house Jessie and Henrietta aroused
everybody. At the Drew place "two old salts," as
Amy sleepily called them from her bedroom window, came rambling in from a taxi-cab and disturbed the repose of the family.

"Where did you leave that *Marigold?*" the
sister demanded from her window. "You boys
go off on that yacht, supposedly to stay a year,
and get back in forty-eight hours. You turn up
like a couple of bad pennies. You——"

"Chop it, Sis," Darry advised. "See if you

can get a bite fixed for a couple of started cast-
aways. The engine went dead on us and we sailed
into Barnegat last night and all hands came home
by train. Mark has the laugh on us."

Fortunately the cook was already downstairs
and Amy put on a negligee and ran down to sit
with the boys in the breakfast room and listen
to the tale of their adventures.

"Oh! But," she said, after a while, "there's
been something doing in this neighborhood, too.
At least, our neighbors have been doing something. Do you know, Darry, Jess is bound to find
that lost girl we were telling you about? Mr.
Norwood goes into court to-day on that Ellison
case, and he admits himself that he has very little
chance of winning without the testimony of Bertha
Blair."

"Fine name," drawled Darry. "Sounds like a
movie actress."

"Let me tell you," Amy said eagerly.

She related how she and Jessie had tried to find
Bertha after hearing what they believed to be the
lost girl's voice out of the air. Darry and Burd
listened with increasing wonder.

"What won't you kids do next?" gasped Darry.

"I wish you wouldn't call us kids. You are as
bad as Belle Ringold," complained his sister.

"Is she hanging around here yet?" demanded
Darry. "I don't want to see that girl. I know

I'm going to say something unpleasant to her yet."

"She is right after you, just the same," Amy said, suddenly giggling. She told about the coming moonlight box-party down the lake.

"We'll go right back to the *Marigold*, Burd," said Darry promptly. "Home is no place for us. But tell us what else you did, Sis."

When Amy had finished her tale her brother was quite serious. Particularly was he anxious to help Jessie, for he thought a good deal of his sister's chum.

"Tell you what," he said, looking at Burd, "we'll hang around long enough to ride over to the stock farm with the girls, sha'n't we?"

"What do you think you can do more than they have done?" asked Burd, with some scorn.

"I have an idea," said Darry Drew slowly. "I think it is a good one. It even beats using that little Hen Haney for a bait. Listen here."

And he proceeded to tell them.

A Radio Trick

CHAPTER XXIV

A RADIO TRICK

JESSIE was of course delighted to see Darry and Burd in Amy's company when her chum appeared on the Norwood premises after breakfast. Jessie had dressed Henrietta, and the child was preening herself in the sun like a peacock. The boys scarcely recognized her.

At once Burd Alling called her the Enchanted Princess. That disturbed little Henrietta but slightly.

"I expect I am a 'chanted princess,'" she admitted gravely. "I expect I am like Cinderella. I know all about her. And the pumpkin and rats and mice was charmed, too. I hope I won't get charmed back again into my old clothes."

"You could not very well help Mrs. Foley in that dress, Henrietta," Jessie suggested.

"No. I suppose not. But if I could just find my cousin Bertha maybe I would not have to help Mrs. Foley any more. Maybe Bertha is rich, and we could hire somebody to take care of Billy Foley and to clean out the kitchen stove."

She was more than eager to ride along with the

others to look for Bertha Blair. As it chanced, Jessie did not have to call for Chapman and the Norwood car when the time to go came. For who should drive up to the house but Mark Stratford, who had come home with Darry and Burd from the yacht cruise and had driven over from Stratfordtown in his powerful car?

It was a tight fit for the six in the racing car, but they squeezed in and drove out through the Parkville road while it was still early morning. Meanwhile Darry had explained his idea to the others, and they were all eager to view the surroundings of the Gandy stock farm.

"If Bertha is there she'll know me if I holler; of course, she will," agreed little Henrietta. "But she never will know me by looking at me. Never!"

"So she'll have to shut her eyes if she wants to know you, will she, kid?" chuckled Burd.

There really did not seem to be any need for the child to call when the party stopped before the closed gate, for there was not any sign of occupancy of either the house or surrounding buildings. The shingled old house offered blank windows to the road, like so many sightless eyes. There were no horses in the stables, for the windows over the box-stalls were all closed. And the tower the girls had marked before seemed deserted as well.

"Just the same, the voice spoke of the red barn

and that silo and those two fallen trees there.
Chapman says the trees must have fallen lately.
And yet there isn't an aerial in sight, as we told
you," said Jessie.

"Let's look around," Darry said, jumping out,
and Burd and Amy went with him. Mark turned
around in the driver's seat to talk with Jessie.

"You know, it's a funny thing that the girl's
name should be Bertha Blair," the young man
said. "I heard you folks talking about her before, and I said something about it to our Mr.
Blair at the factory. He's had a lot of trouble
in his family. Never had any children, he and his
wife, but always wanted 'em."

His younger brother married a girl of whom
the Blair family did not approve. Guess she was
all right, but came from poor kind of folks. And
when the younger Blair died they lost trace of his
wife and a baby girl they had. Funny thing,"
added Mark. "That baby's name was Bertha—
Bertha Blair. When I told the superintendent
something about your looking for such a girl because of a law case, he was much interested. If
you go over there again to the sending station,
tell the superintendent all about her, Miss Jessie."

"I certainly will," promised the Roselawn girl.
"But we haven't even found Bertha yet, and we
are not sure she is here."

Darry and the others had entered the grounds

surrounding the stock farm buildings and they were gone some time. When they came back even Amy seemed despondent.

"I guess we were fooled, Jess," she said. "There is nobody here—not even a caretaker. I guess what we heard over the radio that time was a hoax."

"I don't believe it!" declared Jessie. "I just *feel* that Bertha Blair, little Henrietta's cousin, is somewhere here."

"And maybe she can't get away," said Henrietta. "I'd like to help Bertha run away from that fat woman."

"Let's take the kid in and let her call," suggested Burd.

"Sure you didn't see any aerial, Darry?" Mark asked, showing increased interest in the matter.

"Not a sign," said Drew, shaking his head.

"That tower——"

"Yes. It would make an ideal station. But I went all around it. I can't see the roof, for it is practically flat. And if what I suggested was there, we will have to get above the level of the roof to see it."

Mark suddenly got out and opened his toolbox. He brought forth a pair of lineman's climbers.

"Thought I had 'em here. I'll go up that telegraph pole and see what I can see," and he began to strap them on.

"Good as gold!" cried Burd admiringly. "You have a head on you, young fellow."

"Yes," said Mark dryly. "I was born with it."

He proceeded to the tall telegraph pole and swarmed quickly up it. The others waited, watching him as he surveyed the apparently deserted place from the cross-piece of the pole. By and by he came down.

"It's there, Darry," he said confidently. "Your big idea was all to the good. That folding wireless staff you use on the *Marigold* is repeated right on the top of that tower. When they use the sending set they raise the staff with the antenna and—there you have it."

"Oh! Then she's in the tower!" cried Amy.

"At least, she was in the tower if she sent her message from this station," agreed Darry.

"How shall we find out—how shall we?" cried Amy, excitedly.

"If Mr. Stratford is quite sure that he sees the aerials upon that roof, then I am going to get the tower door open somehow," declared Jessie, with her usual determination.

"It is there, Miss Jessie," Mark assured her.

"Come on, Henrietta," said Jessie, helping the little girl to jump down from the car. "We are going to find your Cousin Bertha if she is here."

"You are real nice to be so int'rusted in Bertha," said Henrietta.

"I am interested in her particularly because Daddy Norwood needs her," admitted the older girl. "Come on now, honey. We'll go up to that tower building and you shout for Bertha just as hard as you can shout. She will know your voice if she doesn't know you in your new dress," and she smiled down at the little girl clinging to her hand.

Just in Time

CHAPTER XXV

JUST IN TIME

IT seemed as though if there really was anybody left in charge of the Gandy house and premises, such a caretaker would have appeared before this to demand of the party of young folks from Roselawn what they wanted. As Jessie Norwood walked up the lane, with little Henrietta by the hand and followed by Darrington Drew, she saw no person at any window or door.

The tower might have been abandoned years before, as far as appearance went. But Mark Stratford's discovery seemed to make it plain that the tower was sometimes in use.

Jessie noted that the tower stood on a knoll behind the house from which vantage the race track some quarter of a mile away might be seen. With good field glasses one might stand in the second story of the tower and see the horses running on the track. Then, if there was a sending radio set in the tower, the reports of races could be broadcasted in secret code to sets tuned to the one in the tower.

Of course, if the radio instrument was so illegally used, it was only so used while the races were being held at the Harrimay Track. Then the folding aerials were raised and made use of. The cry for help that had been broadcasted and which Jessie and Amy had heard might have been sent out from this station some night when Martha Poole or her friends had neglected to shut off the aerial by dropping it flat upon the roof of the tower.

The question now was, had Bertha stolen her way into the tower at that time, or was she held prisoner there? Evidently Martha Poole and Sadie Bothwell were determined to hold the girl until after the court had settled in their favor the Ellison will case.

Jessie and those with her came to the foot of the tower. All the lower windows were boarded up and the door was tightly closed. There were shades at the upper windows, and they fitted tightly.

"You call Bertha, honey," said Jessie. "Tell her we've come to let her out. Did you try that door, Darry?"

"Not much! We don't want to be arrested for trying to commit burglary."

"Shout for Bertha, Henrietta," commanded Jessie.

Immediately the little girl set up a yell that,

as Burd declared, could have scarcely been equaled by a steam calliope.

"Bertha! Bertha Haney! Come out and see my new dress!"

That invitation certainly delighted Amy and Burd. They sat in the car and clung to each other while they laughed. Little Henrietta's face got rosy red while she shouted, and she was very much in earnest.

"Bertha! Bertha Haney! Don't you hear me? I got a new dress! And we've come to take you home. Bertha!"

Suddenly the lower door of the tower opened a crack. An old, old woman, and not at all a pleasant looking woman, appeared at the crack.

"What you want?" she demanded. "Go 'way! Martha Poole didn't send you here."

Jessie spoke up briskly. "We've come to see Bertha. This is her little cousin. You won't refuse to let her see Bertha, will you?"

"There ain't nobody here but a sick girl. She ain't to be let out. She ain't right in her head."

"I guess that is what is the matter with you," said Darry Drew, sternly. He had come nearer, and now, before the woman could shut the door, he thrust his foot between it and the jamb. "We're going to see Bertha Blair. Out of the way!"

He thrust back the door and the old woman

with it. They heard a muffled voice calling from
upstairs. Little Henrietta flashed by the guardian
of the tower and darted upstairs.

"Bertha! Bertha! I'm coming, Bertha! I got
a new dress!"

"You better go up and see what's doing, Jess,"
said Darry. "I'll hold this woman down here."

Jessie was giggling, although it was from
nervousness.

"And I thought you did not want to be considered a burglar?" she said as she passed hastily
in at the door.

"Oh, well, we're in for it now," Darry called
after her. "Be as quick as you can."

Jessie found a door open at the top of the
flight. Henrietta was chattering at top speed
somewhere ahead. The rooms were dark, but
when Jessie found the room in which Henrietta
was, she likewise found a girl bound to a chair in
which she sat, with a towel tied across her mouth
which muffled her speech.

"Here's Bertha! Here's Bertha!" cried Henrietta eagerly.

Jessie had the girl free and the towel off in
half a minute. She saw then that the prisoner
was the girl she and Amy had seen carried away
by Martha Poole and Sadie Bothwell, out of Dogtown Lane.

"Oh, Miss! is this little Hennie? And have you come to take me away?" gasped Bertha.

"Surely. Are you Bertha Blair?"

"Yes, ma'am. Hennie calls me Bertha Haney. For I lived with her mom after my mother died. But my name's Blair."

"My father is Robert Norwood, the lawyer," said Jessie swiftly. "He wants you to testify in court about what you heard when that old man made his will at Mrs. Poole's house."

"Oh! You mean Mr. Abel Ellison? A gentleman came and asked me about that once, and then Mrs. Poole said I'd got to keep my mouth shut about it or she'd put me away somewhere so that I'd never get away."

"So I ran away from her," said Bertha, "and tried to go to Dogtown and see Hennie and the Foleys. Why! wasn't you one of the girls, Miss, that saw Mrs. Poole putting me into that car?"

"Yes," sighed Jessie. "I saw it, but couldn't stop it."

"Well, they brought me right out here, and I've been here ever since. When Mrs. Poole isn't here that old woman comes and keeps me from running away."

"But once," Jessie suggested, "you had a chance to try to send out a cry for help?"

"There's a radio here. They used it one

night. Then I tried to call for help over it. But
they heard me and stopped it at once."

"Just the same, that attempt of yours is what
has brought us here to-day. I will tell you all
about it later. Come, Bertha! We will get you
away from here before Mrs. Poole comes. And
we must take you to the city to see my father at
once."

As they left the tower and the ugly old woman,
they heard the latter calling a number into the
telephone receiver. She was probably trying to
report the outrage to Mrs. Poole.

"But the woman will never dare call the police,"
Darry assured Jessie. "You tell your father all
about it, and he'll know what to do."

"And we must see Daddy Norwood as soon as
possible," the girl said. "I must take Bertha to
him. The case is already in court."

"I'll fix that for you, Miss Jessie," Mark
Stratford said. "I can get you to town just as
quickly as the traffic cops will let me—and they
are all my friends."

Darry considered that he should go, too. So
they dropped Amy and little Henrietta, with Burd
Alling, at Roselawn, and after a word to Momsy,
started like the flight of an arrow in Mark's
powerful car for New York.

Jessie and Bertha Blair had never ridden so
fast before. Mark Stratford knew his car well,

and coaxed it along over the well-oiled roads of Westchester at a speed to make anybody gasp.

But haste was necessary. They knew where the court was, and they arrived there just after the noon recess. Mrs. Norwood had reached her husband's chief clerk by telephone, and he had communicated the news to the lawyer. Mr. Norwood had dragged along the prosecution until the missing witness arrived. Then he introduced Bertha Blair into the witness chair most unexpectedly to McCracken and his clients.

If Mr. Norwood's side of the argument needed any bolstering, this was supplied when Bertha was allowed to tell her story. The judge even advised the girl, or her guardians if she had any, that she had a perfectly good civil case against Martha Poole for imprisoning her in the tower on the Gandy farm.

These matters, however, did not interest Jessie Norwood and her friends much. They had been able to assist Mr. Norwood in an important legal case, and naturally everybody, both old and young, was interested in Bertha Blair, the girl who had been imprisoned. Momsy said she would put on her thinking cap about Bertha's future.

Meanwhile Bertha and little Henrietta went back to the Foleys for a while. Henrietta was bound to be the most important person of her age in all of Dogtown. No other little girl there was the possessor of such finery as she had.

What Mark Stratford had said to Jessie about Superintendent Blair kept recurring to the Roselawn girl, and she felt that she should tell the man who had charge of the Stratford Electric Corporation radio program about the girl who had been rescued from the horsewoman. As we meet Jessie and Amy and Bertha and all their friends in another volume, called "The Radio Girls on the Program; Or, Singing and Reciting at the Sending Station," in all probability Jessie Norwood will do just that.

"You girls," Darry Drew said to Jessie and Amy, "have got more radio stuff in your heads than most fellows I know. Why, you are as good as boys at it."

"I like that!" exclaimed his sister. "Is there anything, I'd like to know, that girls can't beat boys at?"

"One thing," put in Burd Alling solemnly.

"What's that?"

"Killing snakes," said Burd.

"Wrong! Wrong!" cried Jessie, laughing. "You ought to see little Henrietta attack a flock of snakes. She takes the palm."

"Think of it, a little girl like that going after snakes!" murmured Burd. "She must have nerve!"

"She has," declared Jessie. "And she is as clever as can be, too, in spite of her odd way of expressing herself."

"I wonder what they'll do about Bertha Blair," came from Darry.

"She certainly had an adventure," observed Burd. "Maybe the movie people will want her— or the vaudeville managers. They often pick up people like that, who have been in the lime-light."

"I don't think Momsy will allow anything of that sort," returned Jessie. "I'm sure she and Daddy will think up something better."

Suddenly Amy, who was resting comfortably in the porch hammock, leaped to her feet.

"I declare! I forgot!" she cried.

"Forgot what?" came in a chorus from the others.

"Forgot that special concert to-day—that one to be given over the radio by that noted French soprano. You know who I mean—the one with the unpronounceable name."

"Oh, yes!" ejaculated Jessie. "Let me see— what time was it?" She consulted her wrist watch. "I declare! it starts in five minutes."

"Then come on and tune in. I've been think-ing of that concert ever since it was advertised. Miss Gress, the music teacher, heard her sing in Paris and she says she's wonderful. Come on.

Will you boys come along?"

"Might as well," answered Darry. "We haven't anything else to do."

"And I like a good singer," added Burd.

In another moment all were trooping up to Jessie's pretty room where she had her receiving set. The necessary tuning in was soon accomplished and in a minute more all were listening to a song from one of the favorite operas, rendered as only a great singer can render it. And here, for the time being we will say good-bye to the Radio Girls of Roselawn.

THE END

www.ingramcontent.com/pod-product-compliance
Lightning Source LLC
Chambersburg PA
CBHW020803250626
47155CB00003B/1185